The Carver

Fifth Republic Series
Book 2

Penelope Sky

Hartwick Publishing

Hartwick Publishing

The Carver

Copyright © 2025 by Penelope Sky

All rights reserved.

Contents

Chapter 1

Fleur

I arrived at the courthouse on Monday morning. It was overcast, with rain coming and going in waves. With a heavy heart, I walked up the stairs and entered the building to begin my divorce trial. I wore one of the outfits I'd bought for work, a black pencil skirt with a dark blue blouse tucked into the waistband.

My marriage had been over before the paperwork was filed and I'd moved on with a man *way* out of my league, but it still made me somber to divorce a man I'd thought I would be buried next to, someone I'd known for years but who turned out to be a stranger.

I walked down the hallway to find the room where I would meet with Adrien and the judge, but I was stopped by a man in a gray suit, glasses, and a briefcase.

"Fleur?"

"Yes," I said. "How can I help you?"

"I'm Antony." He shook my hand. "I'm your attorney."

"Oh...I didn't ask for an attorney." I didn't think it would be necessary for a simple divorce case. I didn't want Adrien's money, so there was nothing to contest. It would be the smoothest divorce trial ever recorded.

"Bastien Dupont asked me to take your case."

I'd told him my trial was today, but I didn't share any details, like the fact that I didn't have an attorney. That meant he was one step ahead of me, looking out for me when I didn't ask him to. "I—I don't think that's necessary—"

"He's already paid my fee."

"Oh."

He moved to the door and opened it. "Shall we?"

I looked in the open door and saw the back of Adrien's head. He had a man next to him, so I assumed that was his own lawyer. The judge sat at a table that faced Adrien and the empty table beside it—where I would sit with Antony.

I was about to be divorced, and I wasn't even thirty.

Fucking fool.

I held my head high as I walked into the room, not looking at Adrien as I took my seat and crossed my legs. All I had was my purse with me because I didn't know what else to bring. I didn't have a list of things that I wanted, didn't have receipts for anything, didn't have any photographic evidence to use against him to get a bigger sum.

Antony took his seat beside me. "I'll be representing Fleur Laurent for this case."

I felt Adrien stare at the side of my face, felt him look in the hope I would look back.

I ignored him.

"Alright." Judge Alberto got straight to the point. "Let's begin."

Antony started. "Because the marriage ended due to Mr. Laurent's multiple infidelities, Fleur is asking for half of the communal property they've earned throughout their marriage—"

"Whoa, I did not say that." I looked at my lawyer. "I don't want anything."

"You're entitled to it—"

"I don't want it."

Antony continued to look at me, like Bastien had given him instructions that were to be followed.

"Perhaps you should speak to your client in private," Judge Albert said. "Take a recess—"

I looked back at the judge. "I don't want anything—except my clothes and personal belongings that are still at the house. I married him because I loved him, and his punishment is to know he betrayed the only woman who actually loved him for himself. I don't care about his money—and I'll prove it."

Antony released a frustrated sigh, as if he knew he was going to get an earful from Bastien when this was over.

Judge Alberto turned to Adrien and his lawyer. "If you agree to these terms, the matter is settled."

There was a long pause. The lawyer stared at his client.

Adrien stared at the table, looked like he was about to be sick. "She takes half of the estate."

"What?" I asked incredulously.

Adrien wouldn't look at me. "I contest your demands. Take half of the estate."

"What the fuck are you doing?" I looked directly at him now, unsure what was happening. "I said I don't want your money."

"I know you don't," he said quietly. "But I want you to have it."

"Well, I don't want it."

The judge folded his hands and gave a sigh. "I've been in law for nearly forty years, and not once have I seen a marriage that ended through infidelity unfold this way—with the wife not wanting his money, while the husband wants to give it. In my personal opinion, there is still love here, so perhaps this marriage should be given another chance..."

"No." Out of the fucking question.

Adrien gave a sigh.

"I won't take his money." I said it again, put my foot down.

The judge looked at Adrien.

"I don't accept her terms," he said quietly.

The judge closed his folder and brought his hands together. "Then we'll schedule another meeting three weeks from now. Perhaps at that time, you can decide how you want these assets to be divided. This meeting is adjourned."

"What?" I'd come here expecting to finalize a divorce, to be free of Adrien forever, to formally drop my married last name and reclaim my maiden one. Not to hit the brakes on the process and remain in limbo. "This is bullshit."

Antony placed his hand on my shoulder to quiet me.

Adrien and his lawyer walked out.

I was breathing hard, breathing through the rage that I couldn't express in the presence of a judge and security.

"Take the money," Antony said.

"I said, I don't want it."

"Don't you see what he's doing?"

I stilled and turned to him.

"He knows you won't take it, so he can use that to drag this out for a long time."

"Why would he do that?"

"Isn't it obvious?" he asked, his eyes shifting back and forth between mine. "So he can stay married to you."

―――――

When I left the courthouse and descended the steps, I noticed Adrien standing at the curb, clearly waiting for me. He was in a black pea coat and a scarf, his hands in the pockets of his coat.

A quiet rage surged inside me at the sight of him. I walked down the stairs and looked at him head on, the sidewalk quiet because it was lunchtime and most people had already left the courthouse to grab a croissant at a boulangerie.

He met my look, his eyes both tired and defeated.

"Are you fucking kidding me right now?" Despite the rage of my words, I spoke with an even tone, like we were at a fancy dinner party with others seated at our table. "Just when I thought you couldn't make me angrier, you somehow top it."

He continued his stare, not rising to my ire. "Then take the money—"

"I don't want it."

"Then I guess we'll discuss this again in three weeks."

It was one of the few times when I could scream right on the sidewalk. "We may be married on paper, but we're not married in any other aspect. I have someone, and I'm sure my replacement is already in your bed."

"I haven't been with anyone else since you left me."

"So you're only faithful to me after I leave?" I asked incredulously. "That makes a lot of fucking sense."

He stared at me for a while as he considered his next words. "Let's go to a café so we can talk."

"I'm fine standing right here."

"We're both Catholic—"

"God would never punish me for wanting to leave a lying and cheating son of a bitch."

His eyes dropped down in shame, as they should. "Maybe some time apart is good for us. Maybe you need to live your own life, have your own...experiences...and then maybe we can work on this marriage. I understand you're angry with me and want to torture me by fucking around—"

I laughed uproariously. "You think I'm fucking Bastien to make you jealous? Oh, honey. I'm with that man because he's a goddamn hunk. It started off as just us screwing, but he's my man and I'm his woman now. I've moved on."

His eyes lifted again, and the defeat evaporated. I saw a hint of anger there, masked by the hurt jealousy. "So we've been apart for two months, and you're already in another relationship—"

"*Woooooow*." I scoffed because it was ridiculous. "That's rich, Adrien. Bloody fucking rich."

"Those women meant nothing to me."

"As did I. *Clearly*." Our quiet conversation had turned into a shouting match right on the sidewalk. "You're a real piece of work, you know that?"

"I made a mistake."

"One bitch, one time is a mistake. A mistake I could have forgiven if you had been the one who copped to it. But there were twelve different women on your dick, Adrien. And there would have been a hell of a lot more if Cecilia hadn't ratted you out—God bless her soul."

"I promise I'll never do that shit again."

"I hope you mean that for the next woman in your life. Really, I do. Because no woman should have to suffer what you put me through. I loved your parents like my own, I loved your brother like we had the same blood, and now, I've lost all of them. I'm out here alone, and you didn't lose a damn thing."

"My parents still love you, Fleur. My mother screams at me every day to fix this. My father is more disappointed in me than he's ever been. Trust me, they like you a hell of a lot more than they like me right now. I told them I would fix it, that I would get you back."

"That's never going to happen, Adrien. *Ever*."

"You still love me."

"I don't."

"Love doesn't just die that quickly."

"It dies instantly when it's been betrayed. Keep your wealth because I don't want it. You can draw this out for years, but it won't change anything."

"You won't be able to get remarried, so it will change something."

I narrowed my eyes when I heard what he said. I became so angry that I grew still, quiet. When I spoke, my voice was so calm, it was terrifying. "So, after cheating on me and destroying our marriage, your plan is to sabotage my happiness? That's who you are, Adrien? Because if so, then I'm so grateful you cheated on me because now I'm with someone who would never treat me like that." I didn't know where my relationship with Bastien was going, if it would remain frozen in time for months or years, or if it would fizzle out in a couple weeks. But I knew with certainty that Bastien was far more honorable than Adrien would ever be.

He looked away, like he instantly regretted what he'd said. "Fleur, I'm sorry. I just fucking love you, and losing you has made me realize how much. I'm depressed, like you died or something."

"Our marriage did," I said. "And it's time to move on. Stalling the paperwork isn't going to change anything, Adrien. I'm already with someone else now."

"That worries me."

Unsure what that meant, I waited for him to say more.

"You don't know him, Fleur. You don't know him the way the rest of the city does."

"I'm fully aware of who he is and what he does for a living. Because, unlike you, he gives it to me straight. He tells the truth and doesn't care whether you like it. And it's fucking refreshing." No sugarcoating. No gaslighting.

"But you don't understand the ramifications of his position. A lot of people want him dead—so they want you dead. If you're looking to move on and settle down with a husband and a couple kids, he's the worst person you can pick."

"I'm not looking for anything serious right now. The idea of going down that path makes me sick to my stomach."

"You should steer clear of him, regardless. Fleur, this isn't me being jealous. This is me trying to protect you." His jealousy and anger seemed to have faded away, and all that was left was that sincere desperation in his eyes, like he really meant these words. "He's a dangerous guy."

"Bastien would never hurt me."

"But a lot of people want to hurt him. He's got a lot of enemies. A lot of eyes on his back. I stick to petty crime, so I'm not fully immersed in his world, but I know shit gets fucking serious. It's not safe for you."

"It's funny that you say that—because you hurt me far more than he ever could."

Adrien wore the most defeated look I'd ever seen, like my words had struck him harder than a closed fist to his nose. "They call him the Butcher for a reason, Fleur. You're a smart girl, but you don't even need to be smart to know that it's dangerous to live in his world. If you were killed because of it, I'd have to take my own life because I couldn't live with myself, knowing my stupidity directly led to that outcome." His voice had lowered with pained sincerity, like he was begging me. "There are a million guys out there, and you're a fucking bombshell who can have anyone you want. If it's not going to be me, then please, choose someone else. Someone with a normal, boring, safe life."

All the anger I felt for him died, just for a moment, hanging on to the desperation in his voice. The way he spoke to me as a friend, as a confidant, not as the ex who wanted me to take him back.

"I just want you to be safe, Fleur."

I'll be there in a couple minutes, sweetheart.

I sat at the dining table, still in the same pencil skirt and blouse because I'd gone back to work after finishing up at the courthouse. My job at the investment company was posh and sterile, the office renovated on the inside for a modern look, even though it was inside an old building. The adviser I worked for was married with two kids and an overall nice guy. I hadn't spoken to Bastien all day, so when he texted me, it was without preamble. He just said what he wanted without caring if I wanted the same thing.

I did want the same thing, but now there was a weight on my heart.

It was heavy with the warning I shouldn't heed—that I'd left one bad relationship and stepped into a worse one. Worse but for different reasons.

But even if Adrien were right, I wasn't sure if I would ever have the strength to leave. Bastien was one of a kind, and every man who came after him would just be a disappointment. His memory would haunt me into old age.

He let himself into my apartment a moment later, in a long-sleeved black shirt that his muscles stretched out nicely. He wore black jeans and boots, his blond hair a little ruffled from the wind outside. His blue eyes were on me when he walked inside, a giant in my little loft, his subtle smile pulling at my heartstrings.

My mind and heart were at odds with each other, but my heart won the match, lifting me to my feet and stepping into his chest, five inches taller in my heels so my arms could circle his neck.

His hands went straight for my ass and squeezed as he kissed me, giving me a hot kiss with breath and tongue, his hands yanking up my skirt so he could feel my cheeks in his bare hands.

He guided me backward toward the couch in the corner, not breaking his stride as he kissed me, and he lowered me to the couch as he moved on top of me. My skirt was already hiked up, so he pulled down my thong, left the heels on, and then unbuttoned his jeans and tugged them down so he could sink inside me.

I gasped like I'd never felt him before. Never felt a dick so big.

With his jeans just over his ass, he fucked me into the corner of the couch, leaving my blouse on like he wanted me too much to take the time to fully undress. The sight of me alone got him that hard.

"I've been thinking about this pussy all fucking day." No one did dirty talk like he did. I'd never been with a man who talked during sex and pulled it off so effortlessly. It was the depth of his voice, his confidence, the way he said it like he'd done it a hundred times. Even if he did the same with all the others, it still turned me on like fucking crazy.

My ankles locked together around his waist, and I grabbed on to his shoulders, buried under the mountain of his chest, lying there and taking the best dick of my life while he happily gave it. I'd had a long and depressing day, but he turned me on faster than a car accelerated to full speed. I dug my nails into his back as my face moved into his shoulder. The edge of my teeth pressed against his skin as I came.

He gave a masculine moan as his pumps slowed down, the two of us coming together, my ankles pressing into his back while my nails clawed at his shoulders. My makeup was destroyed by the tears I shed, moistening my mascara and making it smear underneath my eyes when I closed them.

He pulled out of me and left the couch before he buttoned his jeans like he had somewhere to be.

"Are you leaving?" I pulled down my skirt and sat upright, composing myself as best I could, as if I hadn't just gotten screwed in the corner of the couch.

"Got shit to do." He fixed his shirt before he looked at me. "Just wanted to make a pit stop. When I said I'd been thinking about that pussy all day, I meant it." He looked at me the same way he had when he'd first walked into the apartment—like he could fuck me again.

I rose on my heels, slightly disappointed that he was about to run off again. He'd never done that before. Whenever he came to me, he always stuck around for at least the night. But the last thing I wanted to do was be clingy.

"My driver will pick you up at eight thirty."

"He will?"

"We'll have dinner. I'll meet you there."

He'd never done that before. "Why don't you just pick me up?"

"Because I have a meeting at the restaurant. Once that's done, we'll have dinner."

He seemed to have this all planned in his head, so I went with it. "If you're busy, we can have dinner tomorrow."

"You're doing it again."

My mouth shut so fast.

"I'm never too busy for you." He moved into me and gave me a quick kiss before he walked out without another word. His heavy footsteps were audible on the rug in the hallway. Then they were gone, and so was he.

His driver picked me up at eight thirty on the dot, pulling up to the curb where I stood in my dress, heels, and coat. He opened the back door for me and drove me toward the Eiffel Tower. As the structure loomed larger, I realized we were close to Bastien's apartment, but then we passed it and went straight to the tower.

I didn't know where we were going.

When the driver pulled straight up to the tower, a group of men was waiting there dressed in all black, looking like a SWAT team even though they carried no visible weapons.

The driver opened the door for me, and I joined the four men, who welcomed me in silence.

"This way." One guy took the lead while the other three formed a perimeter around me, escorting me like I was the president with my own security detail. We approached the base of the tower, bypassed the security everyone else was required to undergo, and I was taken into a private elevator. The three guys stayed behind, while the one in the lead rode in the elevator with me, the box dangling in midair as the cables pulled us up sideways.

I knew there were two restaurants in the Eiffel Tower, so I assumed we were dining at one of them, something I'd never done even though I'd been born and raised in Paris. When we came to a stop and the doors opened, I expected the loud chatter of guests talking while they dined, but it was quiet—like no one was there.

The guy stepped out first and motioned for me to follow him.

We passed the hostess desk and turned toward the main room, a large window against the back wall that showed Paris below. Dozens of tables were covered in white tablecloths, but only one table was in use.

Bastien sat at a table for four, surrounded by three other men while they smoked and drank, the only people inside the restaurant. Bastien's back was to me, so he didn't see me enter the dining room. "London is a fucking joke. After Brian lost his head, it's been pandemonium over there, and

I'm too fucking busy to dabble into that shit. If you want to take it, so be it. But the tariff still applies."

I didn't belong here.

The man who had escorted me into the tower guided me to the other side of the room, where a table for two was positioned against the window. He was gone the second I sat down. A waitress appeared a moment later, bringing me a glass of water along with a bottle of wine. She uncorked it and filled my glass before she left it on the table and disappeared.

The guys kept talking on the other side of the room, the specifics of the deal unclear to me because of the distance between the tables. But it was obvious that Bastien was the one running the show, and the guys took his lead.

A couple minutes later, the meeting seemed to have finished because all the men rose to their feet, shook hands, and they departed, while Bastien remained behind. He put out his cigar in the ashtray before he turned to me and crossed the room, his eyes lit up and playful at the sight of me.

When he reached the table, he leaned down to kiss me before he took the seat across from me. "I'm fucking hungry."

"How come no one else is here?"

"Because I booked the whole place." He looked at the menu the waitress had brought earlier. He turned over his shoulder and called toward the kitchen, "Let's get this going." He faced me again and poured himself a glass of wine. "How'd today go?"

I was still overwhelmed by everything that had just happened, that I was dining in Jules Verne, one of the most iconic restaurants in Paris, because the man I was seeing had booked it for a meeting. The divorce hearing felt like a week ago. "You didn't have to get me a lawyer."

"You should never represent yourself in a trial."

"It's not like I'm on trial for murder."

"It's still a legal matter."

"But he was under the impression that I wanted half of the estate when I don't want anything. So, he must have gotten that information from you."

He absorbed that accusation with no reaction. "Out of principle, you should take it. Just because he earned the money doesn't mean it's not half yours. But more importantly, this divorce will be over much quicker if you just accept it."

My eyes narrowed. "So you know Adrien wants me to take it."

"Antony told me it was in the paperwork he filed. It's obvious he's trying to drag this out."

Bastien hadn't even been in the courtroom, and he'd

figured it out. He didn't even know my husband, but he knew his endgame.

"You don't need his money, not when you've got a much richer man to take care of you. But you should bleed him dry as payback for what he did to you. He obviously cares more about money than you."

"But I cared more about him than I ever cared about money—and that's the point."

"You would rather be righteous than vindictive?"

"Yes. Wouldn't you?"

He stared at me for a while before a smile formed on his lips. "Piss me off, and I'm the most vindictive motherfucker you'll ever meet. If it were me, I'd take him for everything. If it were me, I would wait until he got serious with someone new before I told her what a lying, cheating sack of shit he is. And then I would do it with the next girl...and the next girl...until he dies alone."

He didn't threaten me at all, but the tension in my arms made me feel like he had. He said it all with a smile, but that made his words more terrifying. Adrien warned me Bastien was dangerous, and I was witnessing a hint of that firsthand. "What will you do to me if I piss you off?"

His smile was wiped clean off his face as his eyebrows furrowed at the question. "You're immune to my wrath. All women are."

"But what if I cheated on you? You would do that?" Taking half of what was mine was one thing, but to sabotage Adrien's future happiness was ruthless.

"I'd kill the guy who touched you, but I would do nothing to you."

That answer just made me more uncomfortable. My eyes shifted away from his face to the window, the cold evening seeping through the cracks and hitting my bare skin. The waitress came over to bring our first course, which was lucky timing because I needed a moment to figure out how I felt about all of this.

Bastien stared me down while the waitress served us. He didn't say thank you before she walked away. Just stared hard at my face like his eyes were bullets. When she was gone, he spoke. "I've upset you."

I kept my eyes aimed out the window and ignored the soup placed in front of us.

"What did I say?"

Despite how cold the window was, I was flushed with a searing heat that burned my cheeks. It was the first time I'd felt afraid of him because it was the first time I'd seen a version of him I didn't want to see. "I would like to leave, please." My voice came out quiet, calm, even though I was nothing of the sort.

He just stared at me.

I rose to my feet and grabbed my coat off the back of the chair before I put it on.

He continued to sit there. "Are you going to answer me?"

"I—I don't think we should see each other anymore."

He cocked his head slightly, the flames in his eyes igniting. "Sit down."

"I said, I want to leave—"

"Sit your ass down." He slammed his closed fist against the table, and the plates and silverware made a distinctive clatter. "Now."

I dropped back into the chair, my mouth dry with discomfort. "I asked to leave—"

"You can go after we talk," he said. "Now, tell me what the fuck I said to offend you so deeply."

My eyes went down to the soup again, hot in the jacket.

"Look at me."

I forced my eyes to his.

"Take off the coat."

I obeyed, only because I was smothered in the heat.

"Explain."

I saw the red flags and felt the drums of warning pound in my chest. So afraid of getting hurt again in any capacity, I was steering clear of any chances for regret. "You're dangerous."

He cocked his slightly like he didn't understand. "I'm very fucking dangerous, sweetheart. But I'm not dangerous to you."

"You just said you would kill someone if I fucked them."

"Yeah, I would." He doubled down, didn't backpedal, didn't gaslight me.

"So, I would get someone killed...and I would have to carry that guilt."

"Don't fuck anyone else, and you'll save lives. You're a superhero."

I didn't find this one bit funny. "I'm being serious."

"You aren't the type of person to fuck around, so this hypothetical situation is pointless."

"But everything you said...shows me who you are."

He stared at me for a long time, eyes narrowed and lethal. "Let me tell you who I am, sweetheart. I don't believe in forgiveness or second chances. For those who think they can outsmart me and cross me, I cut them into slices of bacon and feed them to the dogs on the street. My ruthless temper precedes me, and my reputation is its own empire. But there are lines even I don't cross. I would never hurt a woman or a child, for any reason whatsoever. And I would never hurt you, not just because you fall into that category, but because of how deeply I care for you." He stared for several beats, his gaze molten-hot as it burned into mine. "That's who I am. You're the last person on this earth who needs to be afraid of me."

I looked out the window again.

Despite the fact that he was starving, he continued to focus on me and let his food grow cold. "Sweetheart."

I wouldn't look at him.

"I still don't understand the issue here."

I turned back to him. "You're dangerous."

"I'm not dangerous to you." His temper flared. "How many times have I said that?"

"But you're dangerous by association. What happens when someone wants to avenge the person you turned into human bacon? They're going to come after me. I'm the one who's going to be used to get to you. Being on top means everyone below wants to take you down. The target on your back is also on mine. So, yes, you're very fucking dangerous, Bastien."

In silence, he stared at me, his expression hard as a statue.

I hadn't expected dinner to unfold like this. It all happened so fast. "I walk into an empty restaurant, and you're doing a deal right across the room." Adrien's words haunted me too, but I didn't dare say that out loud.

23

Bastien was quiet for a long time. "It's an unspoken rule—families are immune. We don't come for wives or children. It's dishonorable, and no one wants to work with a dishonorable man because he may turn around and do the same to you. Being with me doesn't put you in danger. And even if someone ever tried to start something—" he looked me hard in the eye "—I would never let anything happen to you. I would die for you. I would let my body be pumped with a hundred bullets before you got a single scratch. I would slice my own fucking throat to spare you any discomfort." His eyes shifted back and forth between mine. "You understand me?"

My eyes flicked away again.

"Eyes on me."

I sighed before I looked at him again.

"You were fine with this, and now you aren't. So, where is this coming from?"

I didn't want to say.

He continued to study my face, searching for the answer. "It was that little bitch, wasn't it?"

How the fuck did he do that?

He must have taken my silence as affirmation because he said, "That's the most hypocritical bullshit I've ever heard. You were in far more danger with him than you ever would be with me."

"He steals art. He doesn't deal drugs or move weapons."

He scoffed. "The wealthy appreciate wine and art more than anybody else. Whether you earn your money pushing heroin or selling rifles to criminals, it doesn't change that fact. And they aren't happy that your ex is taking Monets, Picassos, and da Vincis from the people and putting them in rich assholes' shitters. He's pissed off a lot of people, and once they figure out it's him, he's dead."

I breathed quietly, but I felt my adrenaline spike.

"Another thing that he hid from you."

That whole time, I'd thought I was perfectly safe, but now, I realized my husband had had a target on his back while he slept right beside me.

There was a long stretch of silence between us. Bastien seemed to be giving me a moment to process everything he'd said. He stared at me all the while, his usual intensity gone and his eyes dark. "I've said my piece. Now you can go."

I stayed in the chair, feeling the threat of his words press against my throat like a knife.

He looked over his shoulder. "Lorenzo."

The man who had escorted me here came around the corner and approached the table.

"Take her home."

"Of course." He nodded then stepped aside, giving us a moment to say goodbye.

Bastien looked at me again, waiting for me to leave.

"I'll stay—"

"I want you to leave."

It felt like someone had struck me with a baseball bat from behind. It broke my ribs and bruised my lungs. I felt the blood flow in places it shouldn't. The damage was irreversible—exactly like the relationship I'd just destroyed.

Bastien didn't blink. Stared me down like I was one of the people dumb enough to cross him. "*Leave.*"

I had no words. Had no fight. I finally rose to my feet, grabbed my coat, and walked away from his table. Before we rounded the corner to the elevator, I turned back to look at him.

He had angled his head slightly to look out the window. His expression was visible in the reflection—and he looked mad as hell.

Chapter 2

Bastien

The SUV pulled into the warehouse, and I left the back seat and entered the rear of the building. The double doors were open to the next room, the processing facility where we organized all the taxes paid by the dealers in the city.

Cash was everywhere, stacked on tables, workers dropping piles into automatic machines that counted the bills digitally, while guards paced the room with rifles in case anyone slipped a bill into their pocket.

When I entered the room, everyone paused what they were doing to sneak a glance.

I pretended not to notice.

I headed into the next room, where Luca sat with some of the guys, his laptop open on the table. Poker chips were in the center, and it looked like they were playing a hand rather than getting shit done.

"What the fuck are you doing?" I asked when I walked in. "You know taxes are due on the first."

Luca looked away from his cards. "I can't do shit until they're done. You know that."

"They should have been finished hours ago."

"Well, some of the payments were behind."

"Did you take care of it?" I asked.

"I got the money."

"You know what I mean."

Luca nodded to the other guys, telling them to leave.

They filed out of the room and got back to work.

"Bastien, we don't have to cut off a hand every time someone gets out of line."

"I disagree."

"Being a couple hours late isn't a big deal. Shit happens."

"What shit?" I demanded.

"The big storm delayed the shipments. You know this. We're gonna chop people's hands off because of the weather?"

I grabbed a beer from the fridge and took a seat at the head of the table. The cards were still there, so I swiped my arm across the table and sent them flying.

Luca watched me in silence for a while. "What the hell happened?"

"If we got the money, then nothing happened."

"No. What happened to you?" He gave me a glance over. "When did you become the world's biggest asshole?"

"I've always been the world's biggest asshole."

"We disagree on a lot of things, but you've never been an asshole. So what the fuck happened?"

I gave a slight shake of my head then took a drink.

He arrived at the conclusion on his own after he gave it a couple minutes of thought. "So, the baggage was too heavy after all."

"Shut up, Luca."

"I fucking told you—"

"Shut the fuck up!" I yelled so loud that it went silent in the other room, everyone stopping their work because they thought bullets would start to fly. Even Luca flinched at the ire I expressed.

All those times Fleur had thought I yelled at her...she had no fucking idea.

Luca was quiet for a long time, his elbows on the table. "You know you're my boy. You can talk to me."

"I'm good."

"I'm serious."

I drank my beer, unsatisfied with it because it was so fucking weak.

"Tell me what happened."

"No."

Luca gave a sigh. "I'm sorry for the shit I said before. You can talk to me."

"No, you were right," I said. "First time I actually give a shit about a woman, and she doesn't trust me and she's scared of me."

"Scared of you?" he asked incredulously.

I gave a slight shake of my head. "She's scared of me and my world—even though her worthless ex is a part of it too. I've never put this much effort into a woman and received nothing back. Fucking bullshit, man."

He was quiet for a while. "To be fair...she was married for three years, and she's been single for two months. Shit is still raw."

I turned on him.

"That is not me saying I'm right. It's just me giving her a little bit of grace. What are the odds that the guy she saw in the bar is the Butcher? She just wanted some good dick, and she got a criminal kingpin who's been obsessed with her since the moment he saw her. She probably thought it was a one-night stand, and it's turned into a complicated relationship she wasn't looking for. It's a lot."

"I thought you didn't like her."

"I never said I didn't like her. I can't dislike someone I don't know. This is kinda your fault for continuing to expect something that she's said she's not ready for—multiple times. You're used to getting your way because you make shit happen. You can't do that with a woman. It can't be what you want just because you want it."

I said nothing to that, not wanting to admit he was probably right.

"How long has it been since you last spoke to her?"

"Couple days."

"She hasn't said anything?"

She hadn't texted me, and I refused to text her ever again. "No."

"Then it sounds like whatever it was is over."

"Yeah...I guess it is." I wouldn't fight for her anymore. I'd told her if she didn't meet me halfway, I was gone—so I was gone. There was no looking back.

At that moment, my phone lit up with a text—from her.

I looked at the screen, staring at her name for a couple seconds before I looked at the message below.

Can we talk?

It wasn't the message I wanted to see, so I felt my nostrils flare in annoyance. I should just ghost her to show her how little she could mean to me when she was on my bad side, but some inexplicable obligation made me write back. **_No._**

Luca watched me the whole time, watched me slide the phone back into my pocket. "What was that about?"

"Martin. Just wants to make sure the deposit will be ready tomorrow."

He continued to watch me, his eyes suspicious like he didn't believe me, but he didn't call me out on it.

The SUV pulled up to the house and stopped at the curb.

I made the call and listened to the phone ring several times before he finally picked up.

He spoke in a raspy voice, like he'd been dead asleep when the phone rang. It was a number he didn't recognize because he didn't have my direct line, but he answered it anyway because he knew a call in the middle of the night was important. "What is it?"

"Meet me outside."

There was a pause over the line. He didn't ask who I was, like he fucking knew exactly who was calling.

"Don't come out, and I'll break through like last time." I hung up and left the car. The gates in front of his property had been repaired, and the guard on duty stared at me from the other side, motionless in fear like he remembered me from last time. "Open it."

He didn't move an inch, quickly accessing the situation and his options.

"Don't make me pull out my gun."

He moved to the door and hit the button. The gates opened.

I walked onto the property and stopped at the bottom of the stairs near the double doors that led into the house. I wasn't sure how long it would take for Adrien to do his hair and makeup, so I lit up a cigar and enjoyed the cool night air against my skin.

He came out a moment later in his sweatpants and a black sweatshirt, his hair fucked up from sleeping on one side for so long. Hesitation was in his eyes, like meeting me at three in the morning was the last thing he wanted to do.

But at least he'd come out like a man instead of making me hunt him down like a rat.

When he got close, I blew the smoke from my cigar right in his face.

He tried his best not to react to the sting of the smoke, but his eyes watered.

"Be a man and give her the fucking divorce. You stuck your dick in other people—so it's over. Drag it out for twenty years, and she still won't take you back. That woman was too good for you even before you cheated, and we both fucking know it."

He stayed several feet back, arms by his sides, his eyes tired from being jerked awake in the middle of the night.

"And if you interfere in our relationship again, I'll cut off a finger and make you choose which one."

"She deserved to know who you are."

"And she deserved to know who you are, but you failed to tell her. But don't worry about it. I let her know. I let her know that the Aristocrats have wanted you dead for a long time. And something tells me they're getting close in their search."

His face was already pale, but it managed to dim.

I pulled out the cigar and flicked it in his face.

He jerked as the ashes sprayed him. "Jesus."

I watched him brush the ash off his sweats then step on the cigar to make sure it was out. "She's the reason you're still alive—if you're wondering."

I'd just finished a workout at home when she called. It was almost eight in the evening, but I'd skipped my morning workout because I had too much shit on my plate. I stared at her name on the screen and watched it ring, my thumb tempted to hit the green button and take the call, but I didn't.

I let it go to voice mail.

I wasn't sure if she would leave a message, but it was best if she didn't because I would delete it without bothering to listen to it. My temper had flared, and now it burned everything. She was the last person I expected to make me this angry.

Whenever she called or texted in the past, I always answered her in seconds. I proved that she was a priority over everything else, a privilege no one else had. She must have realized what she'd had—and, hopefully, what she'd lost.

She didn't leave a message.

She didn't call again.

I left the phone on the bathroom counter then stepped into the shower. I suspected that was the last time she would contact me. Our white-hot burning passion burst in a crescendo and then turned straight to ash. If I weren't so pissed off, that fact might bother me more, but she'd offended me, a man who wasn't easily offended.

I stepped out of the shower and did a quick towel-dry before I looked at my phone again, wondering if she'd texted whatever she wanted to say. That was the only way for her to get her message across when I refused to speak to her.

But there was nothing from her.

Instead, I had a text from Gerard. ***Fleur is downstairs in the parlor. Shall I send her upstairs?***

I read the message at least twice, feeling the sudden tension in my chest. I hadn't expected her to show up at my house like that. Honestly, I was a bit impressed that she cared enough to fight. With all the times she'd tried to run from me, I was surprised she was the one doing the chasing. ***Tell her to go home.***

I put on my boxers and sweatpants before I stepped into the sitting room. I would spend the evening alone and watch the game, just me and a cool glass of scotch. That was how I'd spent my free time since she'd dumped me in Jules Verne. I wasn't sad she was gone, not when I was still this angry about it.

Gerard texted me again. ***She said you'll have to throw her out yourself.***

I read the message twice, hearing her sass in my head. As if a pail of water had been dumped on my head, the flames of rage were doused for a second before they returned weaker than before.

What would you like me to do, sir?

My heart started to beat a little harder, and I hated that. I hated the way she made me burn in both good and bad ways. I hated the fact that I was actually hard knowing she was there to get me back, that she was there to fight for me like I'd fought so fucking hard for her. "What the fuck is it about this woman?" She was beautiful, but so were all the others. She had great tits and a fine ass, but Paris was the mecca for women like that. I didn't believe in forgiveness or second chances, but there I was, feeling my anger slip through my fingers. **Send her up**. I typed the message without a second thought and hit send before I changed my mind.

I left my phone on the coffee table and sat in the armchair that faced the door, my elbow propped on the armrest, my fingers against my jawline, staring at the door as I waited for her to walk up three flights of stairs or take the elevator to my floor.

My heart rate was always steady in the tensest situations because I didn't register fear or anxiety like most people did. It was the calm that made me uncomfortable.

Her footsteps were audible outside the door. She stopped before she turned the knob, taking a second before she entered the monster's den. She better have something good rehearsed, because I was the judge you didn't want to rule on your case. My patience was minimal and my sympathy nonexistent.

She found the courage to step inside, in black jeans and boots, a gray sweater that exposed one shoulder. She didn't carry herself with the confidence she'd held at the bar when she served assholes like me. She was the one who had come to me, but she moved so slowly and quietly, it was like she didn't want me to notice her.

She closed the door behind her before her eyes found me in the armchair by the fire. We exchanged a long stare, her green eyes showing her intimidation. As if my anger was a ring of fire that surrounded me, she stayed clear of the flames.

I refused to speak first, so I stared her down and waited. My expression must have been severe because she still didn't say anything, like she was contemplating abandoning the mission and fleeing instead.

She took a breath before she approached the sitting area. "I'm sorry..."

I stared at her for several long seconds, expecting a hell of a lot more than that. "You're sorry?"

Her eyes were different, timid in fear, a bit wet from emotion.

"That's it?"

"I've never seen you look like that."

"Because you've never seen me mad." I rose from the armchair.

She immediately flinched, like I would cross the room and break her neck.

I moved around the back of the couch and drew near, but not close enough for her to reach out and touch me, at least ten feet of distance between her hand and my heart. "You came all the way up here, and that's the best you've got?" My arms hung by my sides, and I looked at her with a mixture of rage and disappointment, pissed off at myself for being hard at the sight of her, for wanting to stick my dick in her mouth while she said how damn sorry she was.

She breathed hard, like she'd forgotten that I was a terrifying man you didn't want to cross. "I'm sorry—"

"For what?" I clapped my hands together hard, making a sound so loud it could have shattered the windows. "What the fuck are you sorry for—"

"I'm sorry that I got scared. I'm sorry that I let the worst thoughts get the best of me. I'm sorry that I said I didn't want to see you anymore." Her eyes watered further, on the verge of a flood of tears. "God, I don't want to lose you..." The tears spilled over and streaked down her cheeks like liquid diamonds.

I inhaled a slow breath, feeling the fuel of my flames begin to die down.

"I was scared, but a one-week trial with your ghost has shown me there are worse things to be afraid of." Her eyes remained wet, and new tears cascaded down her cheeks.

Only a truly beautiful woman could cry like that and still look breathtaking. My resentment began to slip from my grasp because my fingers turned soft on the rope. "I told you you're either with me or I'm gone. You made your choice. We didn't even make it past the first course before you dumped me. I've never had to work so hard for a woman just to watch her walk away. Do I look like a man who puts up with that shit?"

They were just tears at first, but her breaths changed as she tried to stop crying.

I was a sick fuck because I liked it. I liked watching her finally show me her damn cards. Finally show me what I meant to her. That she was wrapped around my goddamn finger just the way I was wrapped around hers. That we were in this together whether she liked it or not. "I told you I don't believe in second chances."

She moved into me, her forehead resting against my chin with her face pressed into my neck. Her hands moved to my arms, and she gripped the muscles like I might push her off. "You're the best thing that's ever happened to me." Her warm breaths blanketed my skin as she spoke. Her voice was cracked from the pain in in. Her fingertips trembled slightly against my flesh like she feared this was the end. "Please don't make me go."

I closed my eyes and inhaled a slow breath, feeling a surge of arousal I'd never felt in my life. I'd had good sex, desired beautiful women, explored everything there was to explore. But none of those experiences compared to how I felt now, elicited by this single woman. All I wanted was for her to want me with the intensity that I wanted her.

I slid my hand into her hair, and I forced her head back to look at me.

Her eyes were still wet and dripping in fear, afraid of what I would say next.

"Are you in this with me?"

"Yes."

"Are you sure? Because I'm a dangerous man in a dangerous business, and that's never going to change. I am who I am, and if you want me, you need to accept me. You need to accept that I want all of you to myself, that I don't want to share you or be shared, that I want more than just something casual and easy. I want you to be my woman, I want commitment, I want something more than a week or a month or a year. Maybe forever. Don't forget you aren't the only one who's got a heart on the line. Don't forget you aren't the only one who's risking something. I've never done this before, but I know I want to do it with you. Those are my terms. So, if any of that is disagreeable to you, then get out now and don't waste my fucking time."

The tears stopped, but pools of emotion were still in her eyes. She cupped my jaw, and she rose on her tiptoes like a ballerina to get as close to me as possible, bending over backward to accommodate me the way I'd bent my back so many times. "I've never been more sure of anything in my life."

This woman cast a fucking spell over me because the anger evaporated with the wave of her hand. I should still be livid right now, make her work harder for my pardon, but all I wanted to do was take her to bed and forget the whole thing. I could read people so well no one ever wanted to play poker with me because I cleaned house every single time, and right now, I could read her sincerity like words rather than emotions. The glow in her eyes was as brilliant as the northern lights, ethereal and beautiful. She wore her heart on her sleeve and didn't try to hide her hand from me. She'd finally put her cards on the table and folded. Maybe it would be different this time, maybe it wouldn't. Either way, I was all in. I'd been all in for this woman the second I'd had her. I'd known it was different when I'd left that note after our first night together. With another woman, I would have walked out and never seen her again. But with Fleur, I'd absolutely wanted to see her again.

Why? I had no fucking idea.

I fisted her hair hard as I kept her face on mine. "Show me how sorry you are, sweetheart." I'd wanted to shove my dick into her mouth the second she walked in the door. Wanted to fuck her even in my hottest rage. The magnetism that pulled me to her was impervious to all forms of destruction. "Show me how certain you are." My hand left her hair, and I stepped around her, moving to the armchair by the fireplace before I sat down, my feet bare on the rug, my naked chest feeling the warmth from the flames.

She came around the chair and looked down at me, still fully dressed in her jeans and sweater.

I stared her down and waited for her to make the first move.

Her eyes were still wet, but now that she had a chance to get me back, her tears had ceased. She pulled the gray sweater over her head, revealing a black bra underneath with a single strap. She reached behind her and unclasped it, the material falling to reveal her perfect tits.

I'd missed those tits. The nipples were hard, probably because she was nervous and her skin was cold with her back to the fire. I propped my arm on the armrest, and I touched my jawline as I watched the show from the front row.

She unbuttoned her black jeans then stepped out of her boots, returning to her normal height of a mere five feet. She was a petite little thing. I usually preferred taller women because it was nice not to bend my neck down all the time, but her small stature didn't bother me at all. She was fucking perfect.

When her boots were gone, she pulled off her tight jeans and revealed the little black thong underneath, just a G-string, like she'd put it on in the hope I would see it this evening. She left the thong on before she lowered to her knees in front of me.

I was so fucking hard.

She reached for the waistband of my sweatpants then tugged to get them off.

I lifted my hips to help her, watching her reaction to my rock-hard dick.

She tugged everything to my ankles then inched closer, tits at my knees, looking absolutely fuckable in the glow of the fire. She moved her hands up my thighs before she dipped her head to my lap and started at my balls.

I took an involuntary breath because her lips were so fucking nice on my sac.

She kissed my balls like they were my lips, licked them like they were my dick, and then gently sucked one ball into her mouth and played with it with her tongue.

I closed my eyes for a second as I enjoyed it.

She took her time, like she wasn't in a rush to get me off and move to the next thing. She made it last, like she wanted to be on her knees with my dick in her face. She moved up to my length, parted her lips and flattened her tongue, and then slowly pushed my dick to the back of her throat. She pushed farther than she had before, as if taking as much of my dick as possible was part of her apology. She stilled like she already wanted to gag but held it off like a champ. She moved up and down, slow and steady, making it clear she wanted me to enjoy the journey rather than rush to the finish.

I watched her move up and down, watched her suck my dick as deep as her throat would allow, watched new tears slowly build up in her eyes because of the discomfort from my size. Her soft fingers played with my balls at the same time, giving head so good it was like she was getting paid for it.

My breaths started to accelerate, and I felt the flush in the skin across my chest. Felt the burn in my core because the pleasure was so damn good. I hadn't felt anything but anger this past week, so I hadn't noticed the drought, but now that she ate my dick like a buffet, I realized how much I missed it. "Look at me."

Her eyes moved to mine as she continued to lick her favorite lollipop, pushing far back before she rose up again, always slightly breathless because her opportunities to breathe were limited.

I guided her up and down with my hand in her hair, setting the pace that I wanted her to follow, wishing there were a way that I could subdue my senses so I could enjoy it forever, that I could make her suck my dick for hours without needing to come.

But I already wanted to come—badly.

I'd just had her speed up, but now, my hand steadied her, bringing her back to the tip until she let my dick slap against my stomach. I gently guided her toward me, wanting her on top of me.

She climbed into my lap, her legs straddling my thighs as her hands clutched my shoulders for balance.

I grabbed myself by the base and straightened so she could slide over my length. My hand gripped her hip, and I guided her down, feeling her wet lips open around my head before they took the rest of my length, her ass coming to rest on my balls.

Jesus Christ, how could I forget how good this pussy was?

She cupped my face, and she dipped her head to kiss me, her lips landing softly, like there was a chance I would reject her mouth. She felt my lips for a moment before she kissed me, kissed me gently but with purpose and passion, her breath escaping between my lips and filling my mouth. She ground her hips against me as her fingers reached my hairline, her thumb pressed against the bone in my jaw.

She kissed me harder, circling my neck with her arm to pull me closer, her tongue finding mine. She started to move slowly, rising up only a few inches so she could continue to kiss me.

I moved my hands to her ass and squeezed the cheeks, my dick twitching inside her, harder than I'd ever been in my fucking life. My dick won the battle against my mouth, and I lifted her slightly because I wanted her to ride me fully, to smash that dick with her incredible tightness.

She broke the kiss and moved up and down forcefully, taking me to the tip before she dropped down again, her ass grinding against my balls. It was too much for her and I could see that it hurt, but she pushed forward like a soldier who carried on, even with bullet wounds. Her hands were planted against my chest for balance, and she rocked her hips as she moved, her tight stomach flexed with the muscles under the skin, her tits perked up.

"Tell me you're sorry." I gripped her hips and guided her

with me, my bare feet pressing against the rug to meet her thrusts, to push into that slick paradise.

"I'm sorry."

I spanked her with my big hand. "Again."

She sucked in a breath through her teeth but didn't pause her movements, continuing to ride my dick like her life depended on it. "I'm sorry."

I spanked her again, harder this time to leave a mark. "I didn't hear you."

"*I'm sorry.*" Her eyes watered now, either from the pain or because I was about to make her come. I wasn't sure which.

Coated in sweat and both breathless, we fucked in the chair by the fire, my fingers kneading the muscles of her ass, so fucking turned on by everything she was giving me that I was about to come. But I doubled down and focused on her, knowing it wouldn't be much longer before she slathered my length with cream and came all over me. "Are you gonna leave me again?"

Instead of giving the answer I expected—no—she said something else. "Never."

I liked that answer a lot more than the one I'd thought she would give. I wasn't the kind of man that lived for the chase, so I knew I didn't want her just because she was difficult to capture. But I felt a satisfaction that I'd finally gotten her, that I had her on my dick right now when she could be on someone else's. That we were skin-to-skin, that

47

we'd fucked like lovers rather than strangers since the first time we were together. I never did that shit with anyone, but I wouldn't tell her that.

She was finally there, her pace becoming erratic now that she was on the threshold of a controlled burn. She began to drop down on my dick over and over, her pants turning to moans, her fingertips suddenly sharp as she dug in her nails. Her head rolled back as her eyes closed, putting on the performance of a lifetime, praising the dick that had just lit the fuse of her firework.

I wanted to wait until she was finished to fire off my load, but I was ten inches deep in my favorite pussy and I didn't have the restraint. I gripped her cheeks firmly in my hands as my hard dick stiffened into a metal pipe.

She dug her fingers into my hair, and she drew close when she felt me join her, her tits to my chest. "Bastien..." Her eyes sparkled like stars from the tears, and she gave a moan when she felt me fill her.

My arms circled her waist, and I squeezed as I pressed my face into her neck and finished, stuffing that pussy with an entire round of bullets. I held her there for seconds, but once the tendrils of pleasure loosened, I was aware of how hot and sweaty I was. I rose from the chair and carried her with me, bringing her to the bedroom before I threw her on the bed.

She rolled with the throw, landing on her stomach.

Before she could get up, I was behind her, fisting her hair and pinning her face to the sheets as I lifted her ass to me. I shoved my dick inside her again and propped up my knee before I fucked her like a whore. "Tell me you're sure."

She panted against the sheets, her little pussy taking a ruthless pounding. "I'm sure."

"Sure of what?" I tugged on her hair.

"That I want this." Her words were muffled against the sheets, her back arched, ass in the air, neck bent. "That I want you."

Chapter 3

Fleur

When I woke up, he wasn't there.

I felt the cold sheets beside me and knew he'd been gone a while. My tired eyes peered through the darkness to the crack of light between the doors that led to the sitting room. Then I heard his voice, like he was speaking to someone on the phone. I couldn't make it out, not when he spoke quietly and the doors blocked out most of the sound.

I turned to look at the time on my phone.

It showed 4:08.

Bastien didn't seem to have a sleep routine like the rest of the world. He slept whenever he slept, whether that was in the middle of the day or the middle of the night. It'd been a rough week, and I'd found myself waking up in the middle of the night because of bad dreams and general depression. Those moments were always hard because the loneliness was so fucking bitter.

50

It was nice to wake up and know he was there—even if he was in the other room.

Knowing that I'd fixed what I'd destroyed.

He finished his phone call then gently opened and closed the door, doing his best not to wake me up even though it was too late. He was in his boxers, his muscled frame a shadow in the dark as he came to the bed.

When he moved under the sheets, he realized I was awake. "Did I wake you?"

"No. I just do that sometimes."

"Makes two of us." He got comfortable and placed his forearm under his neck.

I moved into him, using his shoulder as a pillow, my arm snaking over his hard stomach. Even when he was relaxed, his entire torso was solid like it was always flexed. He was warm, as if flames burned underneath his skin. I tucked my leg between his knees and snuggled into him under the sheets, peace settling into my bones when I felt him beside me.

He circled his arm around the small of my back as he hugged me to him, his lips resting against my hairline.

I was dead tired but wide awake, not wanting to let this moment slip away, enjoying the safety of his arms and the comfort of his affection. When I went to sleep, my dreams would contradict reality, and I would suffer in the misery of the lie—that he hadn't taken me back.

51

But I had work in the morning and needed to get some sleep so I wouldn't have raccoon eyes all day. I needed to go by my apartment and change because I couldn't go to the office in jeans. But all I wanted to do was stay awake and savor the man beside me.

He seemed to be wide awake too, judging by the way he breathed.

I pulled away and propped myself on my elbow, trailing my hand up his stomach and over his hard chest. I looked down at his tattoos, studying the dark imagery he wore across his skin, a scythe from the undertaker, a phrase in Latin, the Roman numeral for five, all kinds of stuff that made sense to him and no one else.

He watched me stare at him, moving his hand up to brush my hair out of my face. "You'd look hot with ink."

"I don't think I could pull it off like you can," I said with a slight smile.

"Something small behind your ear. A little something on your hip, like a flower or my name..." He moved his fingers down my back, trailing right over my spine until he slid them up again, grazing the skin.

I looked into his face and expected to see a playful smirk, but he was dead serious.

"Would you get a woman's name tattooed on your arm?"

"Absolutely."

My fingers stilled on his chest because I hadn't expected him to say that. "Do you have a woman's name on your body already?"

Now, he smirked. "Jealous. I like it."

"Not jealous, just wondering."

"Whatever you say, sweetheart."

"How would you feel if I had a man's name tattooed somewhere?"

The playfulness remained in his eyes. "Why would I care about a dead man's name on your body?"

"Dead?" It took me a second to follow what he meant, and once it dawned on me, I gave a sigh. "Yes, that's your solution to everything."

"It's a great solution." His fingers continued to stroke me. Sometimes he would slip his fingers into my hair, touching me with a gentleness that seemed impossible for someone like him to execute. "Fixes everything."

"Maybe I'll get a tattoo someday...but probably not."

"I've left some room on my arm for my wife. If I ever get married, I know that's something I would want."

A lot of things happened in that nanosecond. I was touched by the sweet thing he'd just said, surprised that he'd even pictured a future where he was settled down with a single woman—and I was also jealous. Jealous of whoever it was if it wasn't me. I never wanted to remarry so my rage was senseless, but it dropped like an atomic bomb. "That's romantic."

"I can be pretty romantic when I'm not killing people." The playfulness was still there while he caressed me, looking at me with those blue eyes like he never wanted to look away. His eyes drank me in like I was the Mona Lisa.

"You seem like the kind of man that wouldn't be interested in that."

"There you go again, making assumptions."

"Do criminals care about a house with a white picket fence and kids running around?"

He smirked like I'd made a joke. "No."

"That's all I meant."

"I'm not the kind of guy that says never. I'm not looking to get married and have kids, but if I happened to meet a woman I can't live without, damn right, I'm making her my wife. If she wants to do the kid thing, fine. I'm not going to take that away from her if it's important to her."

"In that scenario, would you leave your line of work?"

"No."

"What if she wanted you to?"

"She would never do that." His fingers stopped brushing me once the conversation shifted. "She wouldn't be my wife if she did. I wouldn't marry a woman unless she accepted all of me, exactly as I am, and trusted me to protect her."

He was deeper and more complex than I'd originally thought, but he was also stubborn and set in his ways. He was like a mountain in that regard. Not even an earthquake would change his position. I didn't want to live in this dangerous world with him, but I didn't want to live in a safe world without him more. "Is that normal? For men like you to have families?"

"It's more than normal—it's common. You think these guys are pushing drugs on the street and moving arms because they want to sit on a pile of money by themselves? They do it because they have a family like everyone else. Want to send their kids to the best schools, leave an estate that will take care of their descendants for generations to come. The line of work is questionable, but the quality of the men behind it is not. There are exceptions to that, obviously, but a lot of men just want to support their families, buy their wife a diamond necklace and maybe one or two for their mistress."

"Because quality men always have mistresses."

"Some of them do, but most of them don't," he said. "I may personally disagree with it, but I'm not one to judge."

I continued to graze his chest with my fingers, marveling at the strength underneath his warm skin. "So, when does the job end? When does a man like you retire?"

"I'll know when the time comes."

"You obviously don't need any money, so you must enjoy it." I wasn't really asking him anything, talking aloud to myself, mostly. It must be the adrenaline, the power, the lifestyle. Bastien didn't seem like the kind of man that could work for someone else. I couldn't see him being a police chief or something along those lines either. He was one of a kind.

My shoulder felt stiff from being propped up during the conversation, so I lay back down and rested on the pillow. "I don't want to go to work tomorrow."

"Then don't go."

"I can't bail. I just got the job."

"You can't get fired, so do whatever you want."

"Well, I like my boss and don't want to let him down. And it was nice of you to get me that job—and let me keep it." Let me keep it after I'd left him in that restaurant. "Blowing it off is a shitty way to show my gratitude."

"You can show your gratitude in other ways." He moved into me under the sheets, pressing his chest against my back as he hooked his arm around my waist and pulled me in tight like I was drifting away. He pressed his face into my hair, and he went still, like he suddenly felt tired enough to fall asleep.

I lay there and felt his chest rise and fall against my back, felt his breaths fall on the back of my neck. Through the crack in the doors, I could tell there was a hint of dawn in the sky, faint but distinct.

I had to wake up in just an hour or two and leave this cozy bed and the sexy man who slept in it—the last thing I wanted to do.

My boss was Robert, a nice guy who wore a different-colored suit to work every day. His desk had a few pictures of his husband and their kids. He liked his coffee black, made small talk but not too much of it, and sent me an email every morning with the tasks he wanted me to complete.

It was way easier than being a bartender.

There were other investment guys in the office too, loud and obnoxious. If I ran into them in the hallway, they chatted with me far longer than they should. After office meetings, they would invite me to lunch, which I always declined. I suspected they had no idea who owned this company and the fact that I was fucking him.

I'd never say anything to Bastien, though, because I still wasn't sure if he would walk in there and kill them all.

I was dead tired with bags under my eyes, but I pushed through the day. I'd only gotten paid once so far, and it was substantially more than I had been making before. For the first time since I'd left Adrien, I actually had money in my account I didn't have to use.

So, I showed up, because I needed this job.

I had access to a lot of accounts to do my job, and it was abundantly clear on my first day that there were a lot of rich people in Paris. And when I say rich, I didn't mean millionaire-rich, but billionaire-rich. Whenever clients would come into the office to meet with Robert or the other investment suits, I knew they were somebody.

It was almost the end of the day, and I kept glancing at the time in the corner of my computer screen, desperate to go home and take a nap. A shower would be nice too because I hadn't had the chance to do so after I'd left Bastien's. My makeup was thrown on in a rush and my hairstyle was a day old, so I didn't look my best. I would be more self-conscious about it if I weren't so fucking tired.

I just wanted to go home.

I was at my desk when I heard a familiar voice outside my office. A voice I'd recognize anywhere because I heard it every night in my dreams. "Half in the Caymans and the other half in Panama. I sent the transaction number to you."

I stared out the open door and listened to his voice. He'd never shown up at the office before. I hadn't thought that was unusual, but since he owned the place, I guess it was. An email remained open on my screen but ignored because I continued to look out the door into the hallway.

Heavy boots against the hardwood were audible, growing louder as he approached my doorway, and then he rounded the corner and appeared, in a black bomber jacket with a black shirt underneath, dark jeans and boots, the black ink of his tattoo visible up his neck. He was the hardest man I'd ever seen, but god, he was so pretty.

He sauntered into the small office and stopped before my desk, his head cocked slightly as he watched me stare at him.

My ass remained glued to the chair because I was paralyzed by how fine he looked. Light came in from the window behind me and brightened his face with a gentle glow. It made the hardness of his jawline more prevalent, his cheekbones more distinct, like they'd been contoured by a makeup artist.

"I'm your man, right?"

I stilled at the venom in his voice.

"Then get your ass up and show it."

I snapped out of my reverie. "Sorry...you're just so hot, I lose my mind a little bit."

The signs of anger left his face, and that handsome smile melted over his mouth like butter. "That's fair."

I left the chair and came around the desk, wearing the black pumps that I'd kicked off under my desk because they hurt like a bitch. I moved into him, sliding my arms over his as they encircled me. I caught his lips with mine and kissed him, really kissed him, not afraid of being caught because the only man who could fire me was the one gripping my ass.

His smell made me lean into him, the scent of rain and body soap, the scent in his sheets, the scent that absorbed into my skin and made me smell like him. The second he was in my presence, my life felt calm, like a slow river outside a cabin in the mountains of Norway, simply tranquil. "I missed you."

He yanked my skirt up over my ass so he could grip one of my cheeks with his bare hand. His massive size blocked the doorway, so if someone walked by, they wouldn't be able to see my bare ass in my black thong. "That's better."

"That's not clingy? I just saw you this morning."

"No. And you better step it up a notch because I'm still mad as hell." He dug his fingers into my ass, and he seemed just a step away from spanking me hard on the ass. "And I'll be mad for a long time."

"Then how about I make you dinner tonight?"

He looked into my eyes so intensely, it was as if he hadn't heard what I said. "I don't want you to cook dinner. I want you on your back and coming around my dick."

A flush erupted through me and seared my flesh like a steak on the skillet. No other man could pull off a statement like that so effortlessly.

"I'll pick you up for dinner at eight. Whatever dress you wear tonight, there better be nothing underneath it." He finally released my ass and pulled the skirt back down over my thong before he gave me a playful spank.

I swallowed, my exhaustion gone when he lit a fire that burned me alive.

He started to move away, like his visit was over.

"What brings you by?"

"Business."

"Why do you have an investment company?"

"A lot of reasons, too many to discuss now." He leaned in and gave me another kiss. "I'll see you at dinner."

"Alright."

He gave me another hard look before he stepped into the hallway and disappeared.

I wore a little black dress, two narrow straps over my shoulders, and black heels, with a coat to keep warm from the cold night air. My nipples were visible through the thin, tight material. Even when my nipples weren't hard, you could still see them, but I suspected when Bastien said he wanted me to wear nothing, he meant literally nothing. It was common for French women not to wear bras, but I always did for the support and the warmth. I did not wear panties either—and I was very aware of that fact.

I approached the curb at the road, my coat buttoned to keep the warmth against my body. The SUV pulled onto the street and came to a stop where I stood. The back door opened, and the behemoth of a man emerged in a buttoned-up shirt with the sleeves pushed to his elbows.

It was the first time I'd seen him in anything but a t-shirt—except for the tuxedo he wore to the gala.

"Hey, sweetheart." He squeezed me to him with a single arm and kissed me. "Get in." He stepped aside and offered his hand to help me inside.

When I stepped up, my dress rose up automatically, and I quickly pulled it down before I took my seat.

Bastien took the seat beside me and looked out the window. "You followed my directions. Good girl."

I felt the smile stretch my mouth as I buckled my safety belt, feeling my face heat, feeling warm everywhere. Aware that I'd flashed my pussy to the entire street, I crossed my legs to give her some dignity.

His hand went to my thigh, his fingers underneath the hem of the dress, lightly caressing my skin. He looked out the window ahead and said nothing more about it, probably because of the presence of the driver.

After a five-minute drive, we arrived at our destination and stopped in front of Septime, a restaurant so close we could have walked, but I was glad we hadn't because I was cold, even in the coat. A Michelin-star restaurant that served dinner in seven courses with wine pairings, it was a fancy place to eat for a weekday evening.

Bastien opened the door for me, helped me out of my coat, and pulled out the chair for me when we got to the table before he sat across from me. The waitress arrived immediately and discussed the menu with us. "Any allergies or aversions?"

"I eat anything," Bastien said. "What about you, sweetheart?"

"No bell peppers, please."

The waitress left to get the meal started.

Bastien sat with his back to the window, his elbows on the table, his ink visible with his sleeves rolled up. "Allergic?"

"No. Just hate them."

He smirked like that was amusing. "I'll remember that."

The waitress arrived with a bottle of water for us to share, along with our first glass of wine for the evening. The first course was served, white asparagus in a cream sauce with a fennel mixture on top.

I didn't touch my food because I was absorbed in the man across from me. His shirt was dark blue, the perfect color to complement his gorgeous eyes. I didn't feel a particular way about tattoos, but he looked so good in them, like a piece of artwork.

His eyes were on mine, maintaining eye contact like it was a sport and he'd already won the gold.

"You're the sexiest man I've ever seen." I felt obligated to explain my stare, to explain what I was thinking. I didn't have that quiet confidence he possessed. I probably just looked like I lacked manners.

He smirked slightly before drinking his wine. He didn't acknowledge the compliment but seemed pleased by it.

"I know you must hear that all the time."

"Actually, I never hear it."

My face tightened as my eyebrows furrowed, because it was so ridiculous it had to be a lie. "What?"

"I'm not around a woman long enough for her to have the opportunity to say anything, and there's not a lot of talking going on anyway." He kept his elbows on the table, the backs of his hands covered in ink too. "And the rest of the time, women like to play hard to get, like that will get my attention. You don't do that—one of the reasons I like you."

"You like the fact that I have no class or game?" I asked incredulously.

His eyes were locked on mine, a hint of amusement there. "I like that you're real. No bullshit. No games. Straight to the point—like me."

It was a compliment I didn't deserve, not after I'd walked out of Jules Verne and left him behind. "I don't know about that."

His stare continued without wavering in intensity. "There's a difference between intentionally misleading someone to get the outcome you want and trying to figure out who you are and what you want when you start your life over."

"For still being mad, you're awfully kind."

"My kindness is volatile and unpredictable. Be grateful when it's here."

My legs were crossed under the table to make sure my girl was tucked in and hidden, but I was aware of the way my nipples felt against the material of my dress. It was a lot warmer inside than it was on the street, but when I wore practically nothing, it wasn't enough.

He glanced down at my chest, as if he could read my thoughts. "Your tits look incredible."

"Because you can practically see them through the dress."

He finished his wine then devoured the first course in a single bite.

The rest of the courses were served, along with the wine each was paired with. Bastien said nothing about any of it, so it was unclear if he enjoyed anything he ate. He normally ate steak when we dined together, but this menu was mostly vegetarian-based. Maybe he'd brought me here because he thought I would like it. If so, that was awfully romantic for a man who ruled a criminal underworld that operated in plain sight.

"Thank you for taking me to dinner."

He drank his wine.

"How long are you going to be mad at me?"

"That depends entirely on you, sweetheart." When the bill arrived, he had his card ready and slipped it inside.

"We don't only have to go to fancy places, you know. I'm fine with something more casual."

"Like what?"

"I don't know, Bo and Mie, McDonald's."

He stilled at what I said, like it was blasphemy. "McDonald's."

"What? It's good."

"I'm not taking you to fucking McDonald's."

"You have me, Bastien. You don't need to impress me with fancy dinners."

"You think I'm trying to impress you?" He cocked his head slightly, on the verge of a scoff. "Boys impress girls with nice dinners. Men impress women by making them come. I take you to places like this because I don't eat horseshit—and I'm not taking my woman to eat horseshit."

"Spoken like a true snob."

"I take that as a compliment."

The waitress came over and grabbed the bill to process in their machine across the room.

Bastien adopted his quiet confidence again and stared at me in silence.

"Why do you have that investment company?" I wanted to change the subject because I didn't enjoy it when he was angry with me. Right now, I needed to do some damage control so he wouldn't change his mind about taking me back. I was also interested in the topic, too, now that I worked there and realized it was a substantial company.

"I make money from criminals through the Fifth Republic. And I make money from wealthy non-criminals through the company. They can put their money in the stock market, but they can also put their money in commercial property, skyscrapers in London, Dubai, New York, places like that. The dealers may avoid prosecution from the government, but they still have to clean their money. The government can steer clear of territories, but they can't hide those kinds of money-related crimes from financial institutions. Other countries and the United Nations would quickly catch wind of what was happening, and that would be bad for business. So they use my company to clean their money, while ordinary citizens use it to grow their wealth. Making the money is one part of the business, but transferring it into usable funds is a separate sector."

I gave a nod in understanding. "I've quickly learned it's a huge enterprise."

"How's Robert treating you?"

"I like him. He's easy to work for."

"He knows you're my woman."

"What does that mean?" I asked playfully. "You threatened him?"

"Just let him know what he's dealing with."

I gave a slight shake of my head. "You didn't need to do that—"

"I offered to make you my whore, but you declined."

"I'm not going to fuck you for money when I'd gladly fuck you for free."

"First rule of business, if you're good at something, never do it for free." The waitress came back with the tab, and he quickly signed it before he shut the folder. "If you'd taken that offer, you'd have the best job in the world—if you ask me." He pulled out his phone and texted his driver.

"As tempting as that sounds, I want you for you, not your money." And at some point, that position might be eliminated, and I would be back to square one. But I didn't dare say that, not when I'd already pushed him to the edge once. My job at the company was solid, and if things didn't work out, he could still do his business without seeing me if he wanted to avoid it.

He rose from the table and grabbed my coat from the coat rack. After he helped me bundle up, he got me into the back seat of the SUV, and we headed toward the Eiffel Tower, where his house was located.

It was a quiet drive, and he was on his phone, texting people, probably about work. Rain pelted the windows and streaked down. I watched the statues and monuments in the streets as we passed. The Eiffel Tower stunned as it danced under its lights.

We arrived at his home and took the elevator to the top floor. The fire was already alive in the hearth like Bastien had told Gerard to prepare it on the way home. I wasn't ready to let go of my coat yet, not when I was still cold, even with the heater on full blast in the back seat.

Bastien entered his bedroom and removed his jeans and button-up. He had a watch on his wrist, and he ditched that too. He returned in his natural state, in gray sweatpants and nothing else.

He came up behind me and locked his thick arms around my body, one over my chest and the other across my stomach. He squeezed me tight against him before he peeled the jacket off my body, exposing my skin to the heat of his body and the flames from the hearth. He dropped the jacket on the floor before he bent his neck and kissed my shoulder, kissed it with a hungry mouth and a demanding tongue. His arms formed bars to a cage that locked tight around me, and he kissed my neck, nipped at my collarbone, devoured me like the cream inside a cannoli.

He pulled down one strap and then the other before he shoved the material down to expose my tits. His big hands gripped them both and squeezed just the way he squeezed my ass, his mouth pressed close to my ear so I could listen to the quiet moan he made as he grabbed me.

I'd fucked around in my early twenties and had the time of my life, but a man had never made me feel as desirable as Bastien. Like he would starve without my kiss, he would writhe in pain if he couldn't make me his. He would howl at the moon in grief. He was a man who could have anyone he wanted, women younger and hotter than me, but his hands shook as he clutched me, as if he was afraid I was the one who would leave.

He grabbed the hem of my dress and yanked it up to expose my ass. Now my dress sat at my waist, just a strip of material that looked like a belt, and he grabbed one of my tits with one hand, while he moved the other between my legs and played with my clit like a pick on a guitar string.

My hips instinctively bucked, and I let out a gasp I'd never heard myself make before. I squirmed in his grasp because it wasn't a slow start to the heat, the stovetop set to low. Instead, it was cranked all the way to high.

He kept me in place, his lips near my ear, playing with me hard and making my knees tremble. "Coke. Heroin. Acid. Nothing compares to this."

I continued to tremble in his hold, continued to gasp because he pushed so hard on my clit that I already wanted to burst. It was a climax he didn't earn, just took. I felt it be ripped from my body like tape from the skin. "No..."

His fingers slowed way down, gently rubbing my nub in circular motions, but that was torturous for the opposite reason. "You want me inside you, sweetheart?"

"Yes." I held on to the arm that was locked over my chest.

"Say please."

"Goddammit, Bastien—"

"*Say please.*"

"How long are you going to punish me?"

"As long as I feel like it." His fingers continued the slow torture. "Now, say it."

I lacked shame, only possessed desperation. "Please..."

"Attagirl." He struck my ass cheek hard with his palm.

I cried out as he lifted me, one arm under my knees with the other behind my shoulders. He hoisted me up, and I was airborne for a second before I landed back in his arms. He cradled me to him and carried me to the bed before he threw me on it.

I bounced before I rolled, not used to being thrown across the bed like a rag doll.

His bottoms were off, and he grabbed me by the ankle, dragging me to him at the edge of the bed before he hooked his arms behind my knees and folded me underneath him like a hot pretzel from the mall. He pushed inside, sheathed in the arousal that had overflowed and seeped to my inner thighs while I'd stood in front of the fire. He gave a victorious moan when he reaped the reward of his labor. He sank fully inside before he ground into me, rubbing his pelvic bone against my clit.

It hurt to take all of it, but his hot skin against my clit lit me up like a firework.

I gripped his wrists and held on as he started to fuck me at the foot of his bed, hard and fast, like a stallion at the beginning of a race.

I lay there and did nothing except take it, watching this six-foot-three monster of a man do all the work, like it was an honor to fuck me when I was the one who should have been fucking his brains out.

I'd been at the finish line when it was just his fingers, but this gorgeous man's fat dick was like magic and pounded pleasure into me with every stroke. I was already there, a mess of tears and tremors, writhing from both the pain and pleasure. "Bastien..."

He moaned as he watched me come for him, his dick just a little harder because he wanted to join me.

"Come inside me."

The cords in his neck tightened like I'd just murmured some dirty talk that turned him on, but I meant the request. Flushed in arousal, his skin shiny with sweat, he gave hard thrusts as I came, and once my high started to fade, he began his final pumps, filling me with a load of his seed.

After a beat, he pulled out then kissed my stomach and the valley between my tits. He sucked each nipple into his mouth then abruptly headed into the bathroom. The shower came on a moment later.

I slowly unfolded my body and felt the strain in my muscles and joints. I turned over, lying on his made bed, my knees toward my chest, ready to fall asleep but too cold to do so. I'd done nothing since we'd walked into his bedroom, but I was exhausted, like I'd been the one on top. It took a surge of strength to leave the bed and step into the bathroom.

His bathroom was far beyond average. His walk-in shower had two showerheads, and his vanity had two sinks and lots of counter space, so much that there was room for a huge vase of flowers between the two sinks. The toilet was in a separate room with a door, away from the shower.

I watched him stand under the warm water and rub the bar of soap over his skin, easily a star in female-friendly porn, and then I stepped into the toilet to do my business. When I came out, I admired the tub, which looked more like one in a spa or a hotel. With gold marble for the foundation and a gold-plated faucet designed in the shape of a rose, the bathroom alone was worth more than a modest apartment in Paris.

The water turned off, and he stepped out and gave himself a quick towel-dry. "Use it if you want."

"Would you join me?"

"The game is coming on, and I've got some work to do."

"Okay. I'll head home."

He'd just wiped down his legs and his stomach when he heard what I said. He stilled and gave me a look that said he was about to snap. "Did I ask you to leave?"

"But you just said—"

"I did not ask you to leave. We can do different things but still be together. Take a bath. Gerard can bring champagne and strawberries."

That sounded heavenly, to sit there in that big tub and not worry about a single thing, listening to the sound of the game, knowing Bastien was just in the other room. But I still felt like I was infringing on his space, and the last thing I wanted to do was overstay my welcome. "I—"

I only got a single word out. Because he looked like he was about to lose it. He didn't say a word, but the hardness in his face was distinct, like fire and lava lurked behind the stare, about to burst free. He'd never yelled at me before, but it seemed like that was about to change.

"Champagne and strawberries would be great."

His temper was immediately sheathed, and he turned to

the vanity and the mirror to comb his damp hair and brush his teeth. "Good."

I sat in the tub for an hour, drinking champagne and eating the chocolate-covered strawberries that his chef made or Gerard had run out and purchased. I wasn't sure which happened, but they were damn good.

The more time I spent at Bastien's place, the less I liked my apartment. There wasn't a big tub in a beautiful bathroom, and there wasn't a beautiful man in it either. Sometimes I heard him yell at the TV when the ref made a call he didn't like. It was abrupt and angry, but hearing his voice from the other room was somehow soothing, just being close to him.

Once all the champagne and strawberries were gone and my skin was pruned, I drained the tub and dried off with the towel he'd used on himself. I returned to his bedroom and realized I didn't have any panties to wear to bed.

I helped myself to one of his t-shirts and grabbed a pair of boxers too, rolling them several times at the waist so they would fit. I had work in the morning, so I should get home to make tomorrow easier. But I didn't want to leave, and I suspected Bastien would snap if I tried.

I moved into the sitting area and saw him blanketed by the light of the TV, his open laptop on the coffee table, a glass of scotch beside it. He was relaxed on the couch, arm over the back of the cushions, his expression hard in consternation because he was into the game.

I stepped into the room, and his eyes immediately shifted from the TV to me. "How was your bath?"

"Fucking heavenly." I took the spot beside him.

His arm immediately dropped around my shoulders, and he pulled me into him, one of his bare feet propped on the coffee table. He held me to him like a teddy bear and watched the rest of the game. There were only a couple minutes left, so I stayed quiet and let him see the outcome.

He seemed to be rooting for Manchester United, because when they won, he said, "That's right, motherfuckers." To avoid the commercials and the commentary, he grabbed the remote and turned off the TV. The fire continued to burn, the flames low because it hadn't been fed in a while.

"You don't strike me as a big sports guy."

"I'm not, but I like to gamble."

"You had money on this game?"

"Ten dimes."

I looked at the fire, unsure what that meant. "Like a dollar?"

A sexy chuckle came from his lips. "A dime is a thousand euros, so ten thousand euros."

"Why gamble when you're a billionaire?"

"It's not about the money but taking money from my boys. I'm a sick fuck like that." He had me cradled into him, my body propped against his hard torso, my cheek on his neck.

When I'd worked as a bartender, I had nowhere to be in the morning, and now I missed that. I didn't have to wake up to an alarm clock and rush out of his house to get to work. I could take my time, have some pancakes and dick before I went home. "I borrowed your boxers...hope you don't mind."

I knew he smirked because it was audible in his voice. "You can keep them as long as I get to keep your panties next time."

"What are you going to do with them?"

"That's my business." He started to get up, and like I was a child who'd fallen asleep in front of the TV, he scooped me up and carried me to bed. Instead of throwing me on the bed the way he did when we were in the heat of the moment, he gently laid me on my side before he dropped his sweatpants, turned off the lights, and joined me under the sheets.

I propped myself up and waited for him to put his phone on the nightstand and get into bed, eager to take my favorite spot—tucked into his side.

His smirk was visible in the dark as he got into bed beside me, opening his arms to accept me against him.

My cheek went to his chest, my leg between his knees, my arm draped over his hard stomach. My apartment was usually cold, so I slept in pants and a sweater because the bedding wasn't enough to keep me warm. I didn't have that problem in this palace, with a man who acted as a furnace, the floors warm from the radiant heat.

I'd never snuggled with Adrien. We always slept on our opposite sides of the bed once our bodies were untangled. We were affectionate in other ways, but cuddling wasn't something we did. His breaths distracted me and I was uncomfortable in some way, but Bastien felt like my favorite pillow.

He lightly trailed his fingers down my back, like he wasn't ready to sleep just yet. "Goodnight, sweetheart." His deep voice was like a purr in the dark, an invisible comfort that made me feel the safest I ever had.

"Goodnight."

Chapter 4

Bastien

Luca sat with me in the back seat of the SUV, driving through the wet streets of Paris until we hit the outskirts where the warehouse was located. His window was cracked so he could enjoy his cigar. "So...how are things with Fleur?"

I rarely mentioned her to Luca and the other guys. Not to hide my relationship, but because I didn't want to listen to any bullshit about it. "We worked it out."

"You did?" He tapped his finger against the cigar so the ash flew away on the air.

"She came back on her hands and knees."

He smirked. "That sounds like one hell of an apology."

"Something like that," I said. "Still thinks I'm mad at her."

"Why are you mad at her?"

"I'm not—just want her to think I am."

He turned away from the window to look at me. "I thought you didn't play games."

"She played games with me first," I said. "It's called payback."

"So, you *are* still mad."

"No," I said with a smile. "Just enjoying watching her make it up to me."

Luca gave a slight nod in understanding. "That does sound fun."

"How are things with Diana?"

"There's nothing going on with Diana."

"You brought her to that gala."

"Doesn't mean shit, and you know it," he said. "You think I'd see someone you fucked before me?"

I gave a shrug. "I don't see what the big deal is."

"Alright," he said. "What if I had already fucked Fleur?"

I stilled at the question because it did bother me—*a lot*. It bothered me that Adrien had fucked her when his dick was unworthy of her royal paradise. The SUV pulled up to the warehouse on the commercial road, barbed wire fencing around the perimeter. There were no cars. "You sure he's here?"

"They hide their cars on the other street."

"Then they won't be able to run."

"What a brilliant plan." He hopped out of the SUV first.

I came around the vehicle, our tactical team already out of their cars and ready to burn this place down on my command.

Luca put out his cigar and crushed it beneath his boot as he released the last cloud of smoke from his mouth. "Let's do this shit."

I headed to the sliding metal door to the warehouse, a smaller door placed inside it on the right, a dead giveaway to criminal activity. I pounded my fist against the door then looked at the camera in the corner. "Here to have a chat with Regis." I stood back from the door, arms crossed over my chest, knowing they were trying to decide their course of action. Did they act completely innocent and lie through their teeth—or did they act guilty and show their hand?

When the door opened a second later, I had my answer.

Regis was there in a black hoodie, the warehouse full of tables that were already packed with the drugs that would be shipped to the port to the west. Paris was the biggest city in the country and the best place to flood the streets with product, but when it came to international shipments, the city was a difficult location because of how central it was. "Bastien, what brings you here?" He approached me with a smile and presented his hand so I could shake it.

I ignored the offer and stepped around him, doing a quick surveillance of the room, the number of guys, and the number of guns. I grabbed an empty chair and dragged it to the center of the room. "Take a seat, Regis."

Luca placed two additional chairs in front of it.

Regis became timid when he breathed in the potent hostility.

"We need to have a chat." I dropped into a chair and sat back before I gestured to the seat across from me.

Luca got comfortable in the other chair, arms folded over his chest.

Regis turned to the men who worked in the facility, the men at the tables halting their packing. He looked at the ones who were armed and shook his head slightly before he sat in the chair across from me.

I stared for a solid minute, letting him drown in my silent wrath. "As much as I hate to sound like a fucking cliché, we can do this the easy way or the hard way. Let me tell you what the easy way is because you already know the outcome of the other option." I reached into my jacket and pulled out the knife I used for all my punishments. "Your left hand."

The warmth he'd exuded earlier had been swallowed by a cold frost. He swallowed, his eyes shifted to Luca before they came back to me, and then he started to sweat. "Bastien, I don't understand—"

"The hard way, then?" I cocked my head slightly.

"I—I just don't understand the problem—"

"Yep," Luca said. "The hard way, it is."

"We know you're intentionally falsifying your profits," I said. "You're cheating the Fifth Republic, and if you're going to cheat the system, then the system no longer needs you."

"I don't know what you're talking about, Bastien." He raised his voice, sounding sincere as his forehead started to collect sweat. "I would never try to cheat you or the Fifth Republic out of their cut—"

"I wonder how deep this deception goes if you can lie to my face like that," I said calmly. "Regis, have you heard of Greenback Investments?"

He started to pale because he knew it was over.

"Of course you have," I said. "And I've heard of it too since I own it. The amount of funds you've deposited into that account is far too high, based on your gross proceeds. You claim you have no other revenue stream, so the only logical explanation for the deposits is foul play. I've calculated the amount that should have been paid to the Fifth Republic and have removed that from your account, so no further action needs to be taken on your part."

He didn't have the strength to look calm anymore. The uneasiness was visible in the slight way he trembled, the way his eyes shifted back and forth like he didn't know whether to look at me or Luca.

I gave a small nod. "Take him."

"Wait, wait, wait." Regis was on his feet. "You said you took the funds from the account, so we're square—"

"I can't do business with someone I don't trust. The Fifth Republic has generously pardoned your crimes and allowed you to earn an honest living in a dishonest field— and you decided to cheat your employer. I can't allow this."

My men started to move in to grab him.

"Wait." He dropped to his knees. "Butcher, take my hand. *Take it*." He yanked up his sleeve so I could cut him right at the wrist and remove his hand from his body, the punishment for thieves. "Please."

"That punishment is reserved for those who come clean," I said. "You did not." I rose to my feet and looked at the men who stared, none of them coming to Regis's aid because they wanted to keep their hands and their necks.

"I abide by your rules and don't use trafficked labor," he said. "So the cost of business is higher. Surely, you must understand that."

"That sounds like an excuse to me," Luca said. "Take him."

My men grabbed him, zip-tied his wrists, and dragged him out of the warehouse and into one of the vehicles.

No one said a word.

I surveyed the men who stared. "Select a replacement by tomorrow, or I'll select one for you."

———————

It was nine in the morning when I walked into BlackBird Coffee, one of my mother's favorite places to have breakfast. I'd been up all night and was dead tired, but I never showed anyone how exhausted I was. Not when it was a sign of weakness.

My mother was already seated at the table with her coffee and raspberry croissant.

I ordered a black coffee at the counter then took the seat across from her. I was dressed down in jeans and a long-sleeved shirt, whereas she was in a taupe cashmere sweater, dark pants, and boots. A gold bracelet was on her wrist, and a diamond necklace hung around her throat. My mother preserved her beauty with every intervention at her disposal, so while she was in her golden years, she looked like she could be in her forties.

I took a drink and let the tension steep like a hot tea.

She didn't want to break the silence first, but she knew I was far more stubborn than she was. "Your brother won't speak to me."

"He'll come around."

"He's not as level-headed as you."

I scoffed. "Then you don't know me that well, Mother."

"But I know your brother better than you do." She drank her café crème then ripped off a piece of her raspberry croissant before she placed it in her mouth. She was thin as a rail, so I knew this was all she would eat for the day, maybe a salad for dinner. She had her own gym at the house, and she'd told me she did nearly two hours of cardio every day. "As you've been estranged from him for many years..."

"I've been estranged from him because of the shit he does —the shit you should care about."

"I support my children in whatever their endeavors may be."

"I bet you'd feel much differently if you had daughters rather than sons." I didn't raise my voice with my mother, tried to be as respectful as possible, but it was hard not to lose my temper sometimes.

"Well, fortunately for me, I don't." She took another bite of her croissant.

"You're a woman. Shouldn't that be enough of a reason?"

She looked down at her coffee and stirred it with her spoon, even though she'd already done that when I sat down. "I would never allow myself to be in that position."

"Not everyone is as privileged as you've been."

Her eyes were elsewhere as she drank her coffee. "I asked you to breakfast because I want to see my son, spend time with you, appreciate the man you've become. But if you're only interested in critiquing my parenting, then perhaps you should go."

She excused all of Godric's behavior, like the issues were merely a matter of opinion rather than right or wrong. It was fucking infuriating. She refused to pass any kind of judgment on his activities, refused to even give an opinion about it.

She interpreted my silence as cooperation. "What's new with you?"

"Nothing but work. But what about you?"

"I've taken up embroidery."

"That's nice." *What the fuck was embroidery?*

"And I've started yoga. There's a new studio down the street from my house. Met a few girls there."

"Good for you, Mom."

She took another bite of her croissant, most of it gone at this point. She sat perfectly straight without the chair for support, behaving like a typical rich French woman, all elegance all the time. "Are you seeing anyone?" She tore another piece off the croissant, her eyes down like she expected me to give the same answer I always gave when she asked this question.

This time, I gave a different response. "I am."

Her eyes flicked up from what she was doing, her fingers still gripping the croissant. "You are?"

"I am," I repeated.

She left the croissant where it lay and wiped her fingers with a napkin, her eyes locked on mine with a hint of elated surprise she did her best to hide. "Is it serious?"

It seemed serious whenever Fleur let her guard down, when she let me fully into her heart and mind. She told me things that other women were too afraid or proud to say, put her cards on the table because she thought she was out of the game. I caught her stare, the depth deeper than the flesh. And when she came back to me and begged for my forgiveness, she finally showed what I meant to her—that I was the best thing that ever happened to her. "Not yet, but we're headed in that direction."

My mother brightened in a way I hadn't seen in a very long time, like the mere possibility of grandkids was enough to light her up like a goddamn Christmas tree. "Tell me about her. What does she do? Do you have a picture of her?"

I chuckled. "Mom, chill. I just said it wasn't serious—"

"*Yet.*" She held up her finger to me in typical mom fashion. "This is the first woman you've mentioned since you left the house. By that fact alone, I know she means a great deal to you. Do you have a picture? I want to see her."

"I don't have any."

"None?" she asked incredulously.

I'd taken some photos of her, but she was asleep at the time, wearing my shirt or nothing at all, photos I took in private. "None that I'm at liberty to share." My mother and I didn't talk about my personal life often, but she knew I was a young man living a bachelor life, and she never pried, probably for her own sanity.

She sidestepped my answer. "Is she beautiful?"

I smiled before I scoffed. "Like you wouldn't believe."

"Blond or brunette? Redhead?"

"She's a brunette. Long brown hair. Green eyes. She's on the shorter side, a little over five feet tall. But what she lacks in height, she makes up in sass."

"Ooh, I love her already," she said. "Does she work? Is she a model?"

"I gave her a job as an assistant at the investment firm."

"What did she do before that?"

"Well..." I knew my mother wouldn't like this part. "She was married, so she didn't work."

"She was married." She said it with abject disapproval. "How old is she?"

"I've never asked. Almost thirty, if I had to guess."

"So, she's already been divorced, and she's not even thirty?"

"Mom, I love you, but you better park that judgment bus."

"I just don't understand how a woman so young—"

"Her husband cheated. So, she left his ass, even when she had nothing, because she's got a spine—*and I like that*."

"But a man doesn't cheat without a reason."

"Mom." My mother was brainwashed by her generation. Still living in a time when everything was the woman's fault, never the man's. A woman's place was in the house, making a home and raising children, not working as a bartender or an assistant at an investment company. I could lie to make my mother like Fleur more, but I didn't give a damn whether my mother liked her or not. I was proud of my woman, that she left her cheating husband because she deserved more, that she would rather do the hard thing than the easy thing. She wouldn't look the other way because she wanted to remain a rich woman. When she said she didn't care about money, she fucking meant it. "He was the problem, not her. And I'm glad he threw her away because I got her."

My mother silenced her other questions and drank her coffee, her previous excitement crushed by the fact that Fleur had already been married.

She was *still* married, but I didn't tell her that.

"If you're happy, then I'm happy for you." It was a diplomatic, insincere statement, but she tried her best to make amends.

"Thank you."

"I've actually been seeing someone myself," she said. "I was introduced to him by a friend."

"Yeah?" I asked. "Tell me about him."

"He's a widower, like me. He's rich, handsome, elegant, interesting. We've gone out to dinner a couple times."

"What's his name?"

"Pierre."

"Is he a good guy?"

"Seems so," she said. "He has a spectacular art collection. And he's quite the chess player."

"Is it serious?"

"Not yet." She smiled. "But it's headed in that direction."

"Then I should meet him. Just in case he thinks he can take advantage of you."

She rolled her eyes. "I'm too old to be taken advantage of, dear."

"You're a very wealthy woman, Mom."

"As is he."

"Even so, just want him to know there's a pit bull in your corner. All you have to do is take off the leash."

She gave a slight shake of her head like the suggestion was ridiculous, but she had a warmth to her eyes like it meant a lot to her that I cared. That I cared enough to bloody my knuckles if it came to it.

I disagreed with her on a lot of things, but she was still my mother, the first woman in my life and, up until recently, the only woman in my life. "Let me know when we can get together."

"Will you bring your special lady?"

I hadn't planned on introducing her to my mother, especially when things were still fairly new, but I wasn't opposed to the idea. "Her name is Fleur, and I'll think about it."

When I woke up, it was six in the evening, and there was a text from Fleur.

I miss you.

It was nice to read first thing, to know your girl was finally wrapped around your finger right where you wanted her. *Yeah? How much?* I was still half asleep, so I fired off my replies without thinking.

A lot.

Not good enough, sweetheart.

I miss feeling you inside me.

I smirked. **That's better. A lot better.**

I want to see you, but I'm afraid you're going to make me beg for it.

It was Friday, so she didn't have to be at her office job first thing in the morning. I was glad to help her, even respected her for wanting honest work, but I would have preferred paying her to fuck me. She'd be on my time all the time. At my beck and call, following orders like everyone else on my payroll. Just the thought made me hard. **I'll always make you beg for it, sweetheart.**

She sent an eye-roll emoji.

Gonna spank your ass for that.

I really backed myself into a corner, didn't I?

Pack a bag for the weekend. My driver will pick you up in thirty mins.

But not you?

I have a dinner. I'd bring her with me, but she'd seemed uncomfortable at the last one. She didn't have to be the woman on my arm for my public outings if she didn't want to be. She would still be my woman at home, and that was what mattered. **But I want you here when I get home.**

Her dots didn't appear for a while.

I wondered if she was thinking about asking to come with me, considered giving it another try. Her dots appeared a moment later. *I'll see you then.*

I felt the sting of disappointment, but I dismissed it the second I felt it because it was unfair to feel any resentment. I'd laid out my terms, and she'd abided by them all so far. *You better be face down, ass up when I walk in.*

I walked into the crowded restaurant, the gold chandeliers hanging from the coffered ceiling, mirrors on the walls reflecting the pendant lights, the vases of purple lilies and white roses underneath the abstract pieces of art.

It was a nice place, but I didn't care how nicely decorated it was. I cared about the food—and the company.

Oscar sat alone at a table for four. His hands were together under his chin as he stared at me from across the room, ornate rings of gold and silver on every single one of his fingers. The table next to him contained his men, sitting there drinking their café crèmes and trying and failing to blend in with everyone else.

I crossed the room full of tables covered in white table-cloths with little vases of white roses and dropped into the chair across from him. He looked indistinguishable from everyone else, in a blazer with a dress shirt underneath, an

Omega watch on his wrist, probably one he'd taken from one of his enemies as a souvenir—and a reminder.

I needed a drink before we got into it. I called the waitress over by simply raising my hand. "Two old-fashioneds."

Oscar gave no objection to the selection. "Heard about Regis."

"Good. Hope everyone has."

"There's always a traitor in your midst. And he'll be replaced by someone else...and then he'll be replaced by someone else. Men are incapable of honor, it seems."

"Couldn't have said it better myself." Oscar was a member of the Aristocrats, an organization of men who belonged to bloodlines of people of great historical significance. As a result, they felt entitled to relics, buildings, artwork, things that now belonged to the Republic of France. It was their intention to reclaim them all. They were fairly harmless— unless you had something they believed belonged to them.

Smart men proactively donated their keepsakes to earn their allegiance, which came in handy when they found themselves in a dire situation. But others refused to give away what they bought or inherited, and if the Aristocrats learned you possessed something they wanted for themselves, you were next on their list. All the rich people of France were well-connected. There were lots of parties and events, and if someone mentioned you had a famous painting or sculpture and they got wind of it— game over.

"What will become of him?" Oscar asked.

"I gave him the opportunity to confess and lose a hand like a thief, but he chose to lie. So my men took him to London and sealed him into the foundation of one of my new buildings." One of the buildings he'd invested in, ironically. They entombed him in concrete, to be a part of my empire forever as a pillar. He wasn't given the chance to say goodbye to his family. His wife would hear about his death from the others.

Oscar didn't react to the horror of what I'd said. "Honesty is always the best policy."

"Not being a thief is the best policy."

He nodded slightly, a hint of a smirk on his lips.

The waitress came over to take our orders.

I didn't look at the menu. "Steak. Rare." Didn't know if they even offered steak, but I was sure they did.

"Same."

The waitress seemed to have dealt with enough sketchy characters to know that she needed to do her job as quietly as possible. She didn't ask any follow-up questions about our sides or additional items. She left at the first opportunity.

"What can I do for you, Oscar?" All the world-renowned artwork and historical pieces that had come into my possession had been handed over to Oscar years ago. My late father had had one of the most powerful paintings in French history, *Liberty Leading the People*, a famous work inspired by the French Revolution, and I'd gifted it to the Aristocrats as a gesture of friendship. We'd been working together ever since, sharing information, killing each other's enemies, and pardoning our allies.

"You're aware that someone has been stealing French artwork for years. Stealing it from museums, from our private residences, even the Louvre. They're putting these pieces on the black market, and despite our best efforts to catch him in the act, we've been unsuccessful."

I kept a poker face of slight indifference, but I saw the problem march over the horizon like a militia.

"As First Emperor of the Fifth Republic, you know exactly who it is because of the taxes and tariffs he pays to you."

I didn't deny it. Kept a straight face and looked him in the eye.

"I want you to tell me who it is."

I continued my stare without a blink, my mind working quickly behind my eyes. I wanted to hand over Adrien on a silver platter as retribution for what he'd done to my woman, for the fact that he was delusional enough to think he actually had another chance with the woman he threw away, because he'd forced her to remain in a marriage she vehemently opposed. But if I gave him up, I knew each of his limbs would be tied to a different car and they would take off in different directions at full speed—ripping him to pieces.

Fleur wouldn't want that. And if she knew I was responsible for it, I would lose her. "We've discussed this before, Oscar. If I give this person up, then none of my associates will trust me to protect their identities. They'll see me as a rat—and rightfully so."

"That son of a bitch has spat in my face." He'd been calm up until that point, but he started to lose his grip.

"I get it."

"I've done a lot of shit for you—"

"As I've done for you. You find him on your own and exact your revenge. I won't stop you. I won't come to his aid, even though I should as his business partner—I'll look the other way."

He stilled just the way a wild cat did before it pounced. "His business is a slap in the face to our people, to our culture. It's a treasonous act against France itself. And you do nothing about it."

"He hasn't violated the rules I've set forth."

"Then you need to change the rules because his actions aren't only criminal—but disrespectful."

I had to admit Adrien's business operations were different from the others, which were focused on drugs, weapons, prostitution, or human organs on the black market. It was far more personal to a lot of people, especially the nobility. It was a problem I hadn't foreseen when I'd started my regime. "What if I were to get him to stop?"

His anger receded, but only subtly.

"Convince him to cease his operations permanently. Would that be agreeable to you?"

He fell into heavy silence, his face contorted into deep consternation. "I also want a list of his buyers."

"That's not going to happen." That would put a target on Adrien's back. He would be hunted for the rest of his short life. "The most I can do is get him to stop."

"Then I want him to help me buy back every piece."

"I'll ask if that's possible." But I doubted it would be. "I'm willing to do this because of our long-standing friendship. I wouldn't do it for someone else, so please remember that." I had motivations of my own—keeping Adrien alive for Fleur's sake.

Oscar finally gave a nod. "You're a good man, Bastien. A better man than your father was."

I wanted to go home to the woman waiting for me, but now I had other matters that required my attention. When I left the restaurant, I headed to Adrien's home, a place with a gate as flimsy as a curtain, with laughable security.

Instead of breaking down the door, I knocked—like a real person.

One of his staff opened the door, an old man who looked like a butler.

"I need to speak to Adrien. Tell him it's Bastien—and it's important."

He nodded in understanding before he opened the door wider to let me into the foyer. "Wait here for a moment, sir." He walked off and disappeared around the corner. His footsteps faded as he headed to the stairs.

I looked at the pictures on the wall and saw one I didn't like.

A picture of Adrien and Fleur on their wedding day.

She looked happy and beautiful, and it made me fucking sick. I'd never been a jealous man, but I'd never had a woman I wanted all to myself, so perhaps I didn't recognize the emotion because I'd never met it in the flesh.

I continued to stare at the picture and debated whether I should destroy it. Smash it into pieces right there in the foyer and let the old man clean up the broken pieces.

Adrien joined me a moment later in sweats and a t-shirt. He was wide awake, so he hadn't been asleep like last time when I'd barged in. He looked at me with a guarded expression, showing a hint of fear, like he didn't know what was about to go down.

He was a handsome guy, but he wasn't built like me. He didn't have my spine or my integrity. He didn't deserve the woman who was now mine, didn't deserve to watch her walk down the aisle to him in that white dress.

"I never know if you're here to kill me or talk," he said.

"Neither do I," I barked. "This is the second time Oscar has given me heat about your operation. I withheld your identity because I'm not a fucking snitch, but I've grown tired of covering for you. This man will not stop until he's got all your vertebrae in a shoebox under his bed. It's only a matter of time before he hits one of your crew and they roll on you. So, this ends now. The business is done."

"Do you stop doing business just because someone threatens you?" he asked incredulously.

"Anyone who's ever threatened me is dead, asshole," I snapped. "You haven't done shit to Oscar, and you know he's been on to you for months. Don't act like we're the same, because we're not the fucking same."

"I can't stop dealing. My livelihood depends on it, and so do the guys in my crew."

"He's coming for you, Adrien. This is the only scenario where you keep your life and your money. Let it go. Get into another business. Retire. You've got better options than waiting for him to cut you into pieces. And understand this—I will not stand in his way. Not even for Fleur, not when I warned you what would happen."

"You're doing this for her?"

"You think I'm doing this because I give a damn?" I scoffed.

"If you're doing this for her, then that means she still cares."

"She cares because she's a bigger man than you'll ever be. But make no mistake—she's all in with me. You tried to scare her off, but she's in my bed right now, waiting for me to come home. If you care about her at all, then you'll walk away with your head still on your shoulders. Because if she knew about this, and like hell would I ever tell her, she would want you to walk away."

Adrien stared at me and said nothing more. Didn't agree to the terms. Stood there and thought it all through like there was something to think about.

"Don't be an idiot."

"You're the Butcher. You're the one who's supposed to monitor this."

"I don't get involved with the bullshit between dealers. You want to kill each other, then go for it. If he walks in here right now, I will not retaliate. I respect his business a hell of a lot more than I respect yours. He wants to preserve the Republic, while you seek to undermine it with your black-market deals. He's not the only one who frowns upon it. If he really wanted to destroy you, he could put a bounty on your head, and people would start to talk. I suspect that's what he'll do next. I told him I would get you to end the business, and the second I tell him that I failed, you're fucked."

He continued to stare at me, his thoughts his own.

"What the fuck is wrong with you?"

"It's all I have," he said simply. "Fleur's gone—"

"You had Fleur and the business, and you still fucked around. You're one of those assholes who's never happy with what he has. Everything could be fucking perfect, and you'd still find something to bitch about. You'll cheat on your next girl and then the next one—"

"Fuck you, you don't know me."

"I see you, Adrien. I fucking see you." I stepped closer and got in his face, forcing him to take a step back like the pussy he was. "Cut the shit and keep your head. And if you aren't willing to do it for yourself, then do it for her." I stepped away and grabbed the wedding picture off the wall, an eleven-by-fourteen frame, threw it against the wall, and made it shatter into pieces. "Pick that shit up— not your butler."

I was angry for the first ten minutes of the drive, fuming in the back seat, infuriated that such a small man had had such a big woman. That someone so pathetic and idiotic had hurt her...made me want to hurt him.

But I didn't want to walk in the door with a chip on my shoulder, so I texted her. *Face down with your ass up, sweetheart. I'll be there in five minutes.*

You're serious?

You're about to find out. Call my bluff and see what happens.

Her dots disappeared.

I pulled up the pictures of her that I'd taken when she wasn't looking. A distraction from my anger, a cold breeze to my fire. I'd taken a picture of her against my chest when she was dead asleep. Another one of her when she'd rolled over to the other side of the bed and kicked away the sheets because she was warm. The top of her ass was visible above the sheet, the small muscles of her back hugging her spine. The curve in her lower back was prominent when she didn't even try. I had another one of her tits because I'd gently pulled the sheet down to expose them, plump and hard, nipples sharp as knives. I flicked through them all, feeling the heat start to burn under my skin from desire rather than rage.

By the time I arrived home, I didn't want to kill anyone.

I walked in, took the elevator to the top floor, and entered my suite. The double doors that led to the bedroom were open, and there she was. Ass in the air with the pride of a raised flag. Her face was in the sheets, her long hair everywhere. Her sex was proudly on display, her subtly pink folds begging for my fat dick.

I pulled my shirt over my head as I approached the bed. "Good girl." I kicked off my boots and dropped my bottoms before my knees hit the bed. When I drew close to her, her back rose with the deep breath she took.

I grabbed the back of her hair like reins to a horse and yanked her up as I guided myself inside her, pushing through her slick folds to sink inside, to absorb her lubrication until my flesh was soaking wet. With a single thrust, I pushed deep inside and listened to her give something between a moan and a cry.

Then I smacked my palm against her ass—hard. "Don't roll your eyes at me again."

She gave another cry, her ass immediately red from where I'd struck her.

"Understand me?" I tugged on her hair, forcing her head so far back she could look up at me.

"Yes—yes."

I relaxed my hold and thrust into her hard, one hand moving to her hip to tug her back into me after every thrust, giving her all my length to claim her as mine. Adrien was at home alone while I was ten inches deep in the woman he'd tossed, and she was fucking wet. "This pussy kills me—every fucking time."

She snuggled into my side, the sheets to her shoulder like she was cold, and she was so still, it was as if she'd already fallen asleep. But then her fingers would move against my skin, she would trace a line that bisected the muscles in my arm or chest, and I knew she was still awake.

"How was dinner?" she asked quietly, her fingers right on the line that separated my biceps from my triceps.

"Bullshit like everything else."

"What did you order?"

"An old-fashioned."

She chuckled. "I meant to eat. A steak?"

"You know me so well, sweetheart."

She shifted back so she could look at me, leaving the protection of my arms as she lay on the pillow.

I turned to face her, the two of us sharing the same pillow. I flattened my hand against her stomach before I slid it up between the swell of her tits. Her body was perfect, and I loved to explore lands that I'd already claimed in my name. "Hungry, sweetheart?"

"A little."

I felt the smirk creep on to my mouth. "I'll give you Gerard's number. That way, you can order food when I'm not here."

"I'm not going to ask your butler to do that."

106

"Why?"

"I don't know... It's presumptuous."

"How is it presumptuous if I'm telling you to do it?"

"It just seems a bit entitled."

"It's not entitled. I want you to be comfortable and have what you need when I'm not around." I reached for my phone on the nightstand and shared his contact information before I texted him myself and let him know I wanted him to serve her if she ever needed anything. "You have something in mind for dinner or chef's choice?"

"I'm fine with McDonald's."

"Chef's choice, it is." I texted him again.

She gave a slight chuckle. "Have you ever had McDonald's?"

"No."

"Never?" she asked incredulously. "So, you were just born a snob?"

I chuckled. "Pretty much."

"We're going there one of these days."

"Not a chance."

"You can't criticize something you've never had."

"Yes, I can. American garbage."

She smirked like she found all of this amusing. "You'll change your mind once you've tried it. Mark my words."

My mind had already left the subject as my fingers explored her body, loving the curve of her waist, the meat on her hip and ass, the muscles in her thigh. She was all woman, from head to toe, voluptuous tits and dark hair.

Her eyes flicked back and forth between mine. "You've already tuned me out, haven't you?" A smile was on her lips like she wasn't the least bit offended that I was more interested in her body than McDonald's.

Her eye makeup was smeared from the sweat and the sheets pressed to her face earlier, but that somehow made her hotter, sexed-up from the way I'd taken her. Her hair was soft in most places but still knotted in others from being fisted by me. I wrapped my arm around the small of her back and dragged her to me as my mouth caught her lips. I kissed her hard because I hadn't kissed her that evening, and I felt a fire so hot it burned me. I rolled on top of her, and her thighs immediately opened to me so I could have her again. I knew her body like my own, and I hooked her knee over my wrist and let my dick head toward her entrance like he knew exactly where it was. Without a break in our kiss, I sank inside her, felt the same warmth and slickness from before, and I filled her until she moaned into my mouth.

I rocked into her, the sheets at my waist, rocking into her slow and steady as I continued to kiss her, loving the way she would bend in every direction I folded her. I loved pussy as much as a man as I had as a teenager, but hers was something else. I'd defeated my addictions years ago, but now I'd picked up a new one.

She cupped my face and then dug her hand into my hair as she breathed into my mouth between kisses. She hooked her arms under my shoulder and clawed at my back with her sharp nails, panting and scratching, her sex gripping me and coating me in the desire she felt for me. "Bastien... I'm falling for you."

Her words didn't halt my movements, didn't interrupt the moment. Only when we were locked together in passion so hot it burned us like a pyre and sent our souls to the heavens did she show who she really was, show how she really felt about me. It was like a safe I had to crack over and over again, a code she changed every few hours. But when that door unlocked, it was worth all the effort—to take another piece of her treasure. "I already fell for you, sweetheart."

We sat at the table together, the fire burning in the hearth because Gerard had started it before he left. She had her dinner, a homemade margherita pizza with a salad and a side of bread from Chez Georges—my favorite bread.

I didn't have an appetite after that steak, so I drank the wine Gerard had brought.

She was in my t-shirt and her panties, eating her dinner like nothing had happened during our lovemaking. That was her playbook, a step forward and then five back, but I let it go because as much as she wanted to pretend it didn't happen, *it did happen.*

But I let her have her way, played along with her game, didn't give that arrogant smirk I was so desperate to show. There'd never been a woman I couldn't have, and I usually had the opposite problem, where they wanted me and I wanted them to leave. This was new territory, and I treated it like a chess game, moving my pawns across the board as I protected my queen—and tried to take her king.

I sat there in my sweatpants and answered a few texts that had come through. My messages went off all hours of the day. The only time it was quiet was between seven and nine in the morning. "Luca wants to meet up for breakfast tomorrow."

"At Holybelly?" she asked.

"Yeah. You in?"

"It's fine if it's just a guys' thing."

"You're my girl, so you're one of the guys."

"Well, I know Luca doesn't care for me."

"I don't care whether he likes you or not."

She looked down at her food and took another bite of her salad, hopping back and forth between the pizza and the

110

salad, clearly enjoying the food because she ate more than I'd ever seen her eat before.

"He'll come around. Give him a chance, and he'll give you a chance."

She continued to eat, her eyes down. "They do have really good pancakes, and I'm not gonna pass that up."

I felt the smile lift the corners of my mouth. "Attagirl."

She put down her fork. "God, I gotta stop eating."

"A lot better than McDonald's, isn't it?"

She rolled her eyes.

"What did I tell you about rolling your eyes?" My tone was still playful, but it didn't take much to turn it around.

"Can I ask you something personal?"

"You can ask me anything, sweetheart."

"Be careful what you wish for..."

I was a closed book to most people I knew. Even with Luca, I didn't share every detail of my life. Some things were kept close to my chest underneath a bulletproof vest. But I was invested in this relationship, and I wanted to prove how trustworthy I was. That meant I would tell her anything about me—good or bad. "I have nothing to hide from you."

She stared at me for several seconds, like she didn't know how to react to a man so honest. "A while ago, you said something about..." Her eyes flicked away like she was embarrassed to get the words out. "That the sex was better than coke, stuff like that."

"It is better than coke."

Her eyes came back to mine. "And you say that based on personal experience...?"

I hadn't expected her to ask me this, and I couldn't read her expression or her tone on the matter. But even if I could, I wouldn't lie to give her the answer she wanted. No matter how much I wanted her, I didn't want a woman who couldn't accept me, the man I was at every stage of my life. "Yes."

She gave no reaction to that, like she needed more time to absorb my answer.

"Heroin. Acid. Everything in between, I've done it all."

She took a breath and then gave a slow nod. "You don't strike me as someone who does drugs."

"I don't do drugs. I've been clean for thirteen years."

"Oh, I see."

"Booze, cigars, and pussy are my vices now. But yours is something else." I remained confident in the conversation, accepting whatever the outcome would be. When she left me, I'd given her another chance, but I wouldn't be giving another one.

"That must have been hard for you."

"I have an addictive personality, but I also have the discipline of a motherfucker, so..."

"How long were you on drugs—"

"Is this a problem for you?"

She stilled at the question.

"Because if it is, I'm not going to get deeper into it." It was a dark time in my life. I wasn't in the mood to skip down memory lane unless she would be with me at the end of it.

"Of course I don't have a problem with it." Her voice was slightly emotional as she spoke, like the question actually hurt her. "Thirteen years is a long time. You should be proud."

I continued to study her, to make sure she wasn't feeding me bullshit on a spoon. "I got into it when I was eighteen. Started off small, and before I knew it, I wasn't myself unless I was on a bunch of shit. It was part of my world, so I didn't think much of it. But then I made some mistakes, did a lot of stupid shit, and I realized I couldn't be a man if I was going to act like a boy. The epiphany was enough to make me stop. Truth be told, you can't run drugs if they're running you. You can't be a dealer if you're a buyer. You can't be a boss if you're at the mercy of anyone—or anything."

She held my gaze like she was enraptured in it.

"But that experience has been essential to my profession now. I know how my dealers think. I know how my buyers think. I can tell the difference between real shit and fake shit just by smelling it. You can't fool me—and everyone knows it."

She gave a slight nod. "I can see that."

I wanted to reach for a cigar at that moment because I'd suddenly become tense, but it was rude to light up when she was eating her dinner.

"Thank you for sharing that with me."

I'd thought the truth would chase her off, but she was still there, still looking at me exactly the same.

"And thank you for being honest. It means a lot to me."

"Honesty is what you'll get from me—for better or worse."

"And that's more refreshing than you'll ever know." She said it with a sigh, like Adrien's lies and infidelity still pissed her off, even when she was in a safe and committed relationship with me. "Can I ask you something else?"

"I said you can ask me anything, sweetheart. Pick a chapter, and I'll flip to the page."

"Why are you willing to be so open with me?" It was obvious that wasn't her original question.

"Because you said the only way you would consider being in a relationship again was if it was with someone who was honest. Well, I'm as honest as it fucking gets. Ask me anything, and I'll tell you. Ask me how I feel about you, and I'll give you the truth—but make sure you're ready to hear it."

Her stare continued, poignant and emotional but also timid and guarded, like she read between the lines and was afraid of what she saw. She swallowed, and her eyes flicked away for a second.

"Pick a chapter."

She was quiet for a while, the remains of her feast left on the plates, just one slice left and a few leaves of greens from her salad. She stared out the window for nearly a minute before she looked at me again. "You told me there are rules that everyone must follow, that no women can be trafficked or hurt in this line of work. You seem to be passionate about it...and I just wonder why."

That was not the question I'd expected. I'd anticipated something more personal, like if I'd ever been unfaithful to a woman, how many people I'd killed, something along those lines. It was a heavy question with an even heavier answer, something I'd never told anyone—not even my own mother.

She watched me for a while and seemed to realize she'd struck a nerve. "You don't have to answer the question."

"I'll answer it. Just not tonight."

Her eyes softened with emotion, like she instinctively knew I didn't want to deceive her or hide a horrible truth. However, the story was unspeakable, and to put it into words again was to relive it—and that was something I'd thought I wouldn't have to relive. "Of course."

Memories hung in my mind's eye like wisps of smoke, but eventually, the tendrils floated away and rose to the ceiling until they dissipated. My eyes were out the window for nearly a minute before I looked at her again, grateful she'd given me the grace to sidestep the question. "Any other questions?"

She moved her plate away, not having the room to finish the last slice. Her elbows moved to the table, and her hands came together as she considered the next question she wanted to load into the barrel. "Were you with anyone else during that week apart?"

My initial reaction was a smirk because the question was ludicrous—and sad. My eyes stayed on hers as I felt the smile slowly leave my mouth. "I'm sorry that you even have to ask that."

"I didn't mean to offend you."

"You didn't. I know I'm not the reason you asked it." She asked it because some boy pretended to be a man and did her dirty. Because someone had shaken her faith in men. "The answer to your question is no. I've been all in with you from the very beginning. A fight doesn't change that."

"But I said I didn't want to see you anymore."

"Still doesn't change anything, sweetheart." Maybe if a month or two had passed and we didn't speak, things would have been different. But during that week, I was so pissed off, I didn't recall even looking at another woman. "I'm not going to ask you the same because I already know the answer." Not because I'd had my men tail her, but because I knew she'd wanted me even when she pushed me away.

Her eyes dropped momentarily, like she was ashamed that she didn't reciprocate the unwavering faith I placed in her. "I'm still sorry about all of that."

"Good." I liked it when she was apologetic, when she was afraid that one wrong move could make me walk away. She was more affectionate, and whatever her fears or objections were, they were silenced. She'd had all the power in the relationship when we met, but now I had it.

"How long are you going to be mad at me?"

"As long as I want."

She played with her hands, nervous, like she actually believed the threat of my words.

"Any other questions?"

After a stretch of silence, she shook her head. "No."

"Then let's go to bed." I'd woken up just six hours ago, so I wasn't ready for bed, but I would lie with her until she fell asleep before I did some work on my laptop and had a couple of drinks in front of the fireplace.

She finished off the rest of her wine before she joined me in the bedroom, still wearing my shirt as a blanket. It was the first time she'd brought a bag with her, so she washed her face and did her nighttime routine in the bathroom, brushing her teeth and using her skin care products. When she came to bed with no clothes, a clean face, and brushed hair, she was irresistible. When she did her makeup in a smoky look and wore a black dress, she was sexy as hell. And when she looked like this, she was sexy as hell too. It was like an outfit change, neither one better than the other.

Once she was in bed, she was all over me, clinging to me like I was the flames in the hearth. My shoulder became her favorite pillow, and she hugged me under the sheets, fingers resting where my ribs sat beneath the skin and muscle.

I lay there for a while and stared at the ceiling, the question she'd asked coming back to me. It was easy to forget most things, to move forward in life and never look back. But some events stuck with you forever—like a scar.

Chapter 5

Bastien

Eighteen Years Ago

Winter had struck the City of Light, and snow covered the sidewalk and streets. I looked out the front window into the night, seeing the gleam of the snow on the opposite sidewalk. It was so cold I could see the frost in the corners.

"What are you looking at?"

I heard my brother's voice from behind me but didn't turn to look at him. "Snow."

"Snow." It was a single word, but it was packed with incredulity. "You're staring at the window so hard, I assumed there was a naked woman across the street."

"Get down here." Father's voice came from the parlor downstairs.

"See you later, perv."

I turned to look at Godric, but I only saw his back as he stepped out of the room.

Father's voice called again. "Both of you."

I heard Godric's steps halt on the landing instead of hurrying down the stairs. It took him a moment to continue and head to the first floor, where our father waited.

I made my move a moment later, unsure what my father wanted from us at this time of night. As I drew closer, I heard Godric and my father speaking from the parlor.

"Why does he have to come?" Godric asked in a quiet voice.

"Because he's your brother—and my son."

"But he doesn't belong here."

"*Godric.*"

I stilled on the stairs and gripped the banister, feeling ostracized in my own home. Godric and Father had always been close. I just assumed it was because Godric was older than me, the eldest son. But sometimes I wondered if it was more than that.

"You don't need him when you have me," Godric continued. "He's not cut out for this."

My brother and I used to be close when we were younger, but a couple years ago, everything changed. My best friend disappeared overnight, and he kept me at arm's length. He struck me down with insults. Every time I asked what the hell I'd done to incite this hatred, he never gave an answer. Eventually, I stopped asking and accepted this was the way it would be. My father prepared him to take over the business, and I stayed home with our mother.

My father left the parlor and approached the stairs. "Bastien, get your ass down here—" He stopped when he spotted me at the bottom of the stairs, clearly eavesdropping on the conversation.

I didn't pretend otherwise, and he didn't seem to care either way.

His eyes were glazed over like usual, like he was thinking about something else besides the two of us. "Grab your coat and your gloves."

"Where are we going?"

"I gave you an order. Now, follow it." He returned to the parlor where Godric remained.

I went to the coatrack and grabbed my things. I put on my heavy boots and then pulled the beanie over my head because I wasn't sure if we would be outside in the cold.

Father and Godric walked to the front of the house where the main door was, their voices growing distant.

"Why do you need him when you have me?" Godric asked. "I'm your firstborn son."

"Godric." He didn't raise his voice, but his tone showed how short his fuse was. "Trust takes months to earn among friends, years among strangers. It takes nothing among brothers. Don't ever forget that."

I crossed the room and joined them in the entryway, and Godric was red in the face. Red like he wanted to scream and accept the beating that it would cost him. But he found the restraint, and then his eyes shifted to me.

He hated me.

Father pulled on his coat and opened the door to step into the night. "Let's go, boys." The line of blacked-out SUVs was already parked outside the gate to take us wherever we needed to go. A gust of ice-cold air entered the warm home and struck me in the face.

Godric maintained his angry stare.

I approached him, mirroring the hate he felt for me. There were so many things I wanted to say to him, that I didn't trust him not to stab me in the back on Christmas morning. But it was a relationship that had already been burned at the stake. Ashes couldn't harden back into bones. We would never rebuild what we'd lost, and we both knew it.

So I wouldn't waste my breath.

"Don't do it."

I walked past him and shoved him so hard in the shoulder he stumbled back into the wall. "Fuck off." I stepped into the night, down the steps, and past the gate.

My father rolled down the window. "Get in."

I opened the back door and got into the seat next to the window.

Godric came out seconds later and approached the car.

"In the back," Father said. Then he hit the button on his side and rolled up the window.

Godric halted on the spot, snow falling down around him, staring at the window even though all he could see was his own reflection. His face contorted into boiling anger, but he didn't act on it and headed to the SUV parked behind us.

We took off, a line of cars moving through the quiet streets of Paris.

I still didn't know where we were going, but I wouldn't ask a second time.

The first few minutes were spent in silence. My father was on his phone, texting and doing emails, oblivious to me beside him in the backseat. He finally placed the phone in the inside pocket of his coat. "You're fifteen now, Bastien. Our society still thinks of you as a boy, but for a Dupont, you're a man. It's time you learn the business."

My parents never mentioned the business around us. It was an open secret, my father's criminal enterprise. But from the conversations I overheard and the information I'd inadvertently gathered, my father was one of the biggest drug dealers in France. He moved his product from the city to the port and distributed it elsewhere. My father was powerful and terrifying, judging by the way he screamed on the phone in the middle of the night and jerked me awake. It explained why Godric had changed so much.

Once he was part of the business, he became as cold and cruel as our father.

"What if I don't want to learn the business?"

My father slowly turned to regard me, his eyes filled with anger and disappointment. "This business is your bloodline. You're the third generation to be a part of it. I would share it with my brother if he were still alive."

"Doesn't seem like Godric wants me to be part of it."

"He'll feel differently once I'm gone." He looked out the window once again and watched the snow fall.

I stared at the side of his face, equally afraid and desperate for his approval. My father had been a constant figure in my life, but I still felt like I didn't know him. Sometimes I saw him with my mother—and sometimes I saw him with other women. My father never told me to keep my mouth shut, but I knew there would be a punishment if I didn't. "What do you want me to do?"

"You'll see."

We spent the rest of the drive in silence, traveling through the quiet streets until we arrived at the outskirts of the city. Instead of the beautiful spires of the churches and the lights of the Eiffel Tower, we entered the slums, graffiti on the walls, barbed wire around buildings, and turned into a compound behind a solid gate and concrete wall.

We pulled into the large complex with multiple warehouses, guards on duty carrying rifles, snow on the ground and on the roofs of buildings. We hopped out of the car, and the guards said nothing to my father, barely acknowledged him.

Godric left the car and caught up to us.

My father ignored him. "Come with me, Bastien."

I kept a straight face, but I was nervous. Nervous for what, I wasn't sure.

Godric's piercing stare was locked on my face.

Father led the way, entering the first warehouse. It had a sliding door like a garage, but a small door was inside that one, and my father knocked before the door was unlocked and we stepped inside.

The room was full of tables covered in nondescript packages stacked on top of one another. Girls were working there, girls my age, and they seemed to be processing the drugs in one section, bagging it in another, and then weighing those bags before they were placed in a plastic tub on a pallet against the wall.

Not a single girl looked up from her work, even though they knew we were there. It was midnight, and they were working under the light from the overhead lamps, fulfilling the packages like they were in a time crunch.

My father walked up to one of the tables, and the girls acted like they didn't see him. He scooped his hand into the tub of white powder and let it seep from the spaces between his fingers, treating it like sand on the beach during a vacation. "We process a million pounds a week." He moved away from the table.

I stayed and looked at the cocaine sitting there before I lifted my gaze to look at the girls.

They all continued to work. Except for one.

A brunette with green eyes looked at me with a mixture of fear and comfort—because she knew me.

I couldn't remember her name, but I knew her face. Instead of us going to private school like the children of other rich families we knew, our father sent us to public school because he wanted us to know real people and the real world. Neither of my parents cared about higher education or university. When Godric had said he wanted to be a veterinarian, neither of my parents was impressed by that aspiration.

I remembered her because she'd gone missing a couple years ago. Her face was plastered on posters all through the hallways at school. No one knew what happened to her, and after a few months with no leads, everyone forgot about it.

I'd never given it much thought because I didn't know her personally.

Judging by the look in her eyes, she remembered me as well as I remembered her.

"Bastien."

I turned at my father's voice and broke eye contact with the girl from school. I crossed the room, my mind in a daze, and came to his side.

Godric continued to give me his ruthless stare.

He was three years older than me, but maybe he remembered her too?

My father showed me the other processing lines, the girls packing the different drugs and weighing them to be uniform before they were packaged and ready for distribution. It was more than cocaine. It was heroin too.

My father took me into a different warehouse, and this seemed to be the office space where numbers were calculated and shipping routes were designated, because it held tables with laptops. The rest of the warehouse was completely empty.

"Where do the girls go when they're done?" I asked.

Godric stared at me.

"They're never done." My father grabbed a folder and pulled up a chair to one of the tables. "Sit."

"They must sleep and eat, right?" I asked.

"That's what the other warehouses are for, son." He opened the folder and pulled out the papers. "Now, sit."

I fell into the chair, the realization smacking me in the face. The girls never left. That meant the girl had been here since she'd disappeared...which was two years ago. That meant she had only been thirteen at the time.

Godric sat in the other chair, arms across his chest, continuing to give me that angry stare.

I understood my father was a drug kingpin, but producing and distributing drugs never sounded like that big of a deal to me. It seemed like a victimless crime, but now, I realized that wasn't the case. Those women worked to process the drugs that we sold for millions and paid for our beautiful homes, cars, staff, and yachts. And then I felt like shit, absolute shit. "I don't understand."

"I'm about to explain it all to you, son."

"The girls... Where do they come from?" I knew where one came from, but what about the rest?

My father gave an irritated sigh as he looked at me. "They aren't important. They do their job, and they do it well."

"One of those girls is my age."

"She just looks young—"

"I know she's my age because I went to school with her," I said. "I remember the day she went missing."

Godric shook his head. "I told you."

My father gave him a vicious stare like he might slap him on the spot. It lingered for a long time before Godric finally looked away. My father looked at me again. "Bastien, it is what it is. Forget about it."

"Forget about it?" Her parents were looking for her, and I knew where she was. Those other girls probably had families too, families that would never know what happened to their daughters or their sisters. "Why don't we hire someone to do this—"

"Because you can't hire someone to keep their mouth shut," he snapped. "This is the only way."

"So, they're just stuck here until they die?" I asked in disbelief. "Working for the rest of their lives and sleeping in a warehouse like it's a chicken coop?"

Godric gave a shake of his head but bit back the words he'd already spoken.

My father raised his hand in frustration. "Forget about the girls, alright?" He slid the papers toward me. "You need to learn how to run the business, who our distributors are, how to maintain order in a lawless profession. This is the business that puts food on the table for all four of us." He flipped to the page that showed the monthly revenue after costs. It was a number bigger than any I'd ever seen. "The girls don't matter." He pressed his finger into the number. "This is what matters. And this is what you and your brother will split when I'm gone."

In a different circumstance, I would have been impressed by that number like anyone else. But now it meant nothing to me, not when it was earned off the backs of underage girls who were too scared to fight or run. "I don't want it." I directed my gaze away from the page and looked at my father. "I want nothing to do with this."

My father slowly sat back in his chair and regarded me like a stranger rather than his son. "What did you just say?"

"I don't want it," I repeated. "Godric can have it."

Godric stared at me before he shifted his look to his father.

"I want you both to run it—"

"I don't want it."

He slammed his hand on the table and made it bounce off the floor. "Interrupt me again, boy. See what the fuck happens."

I gave a small jerk at his outburst. The room went quiet, far quieter than it'd been just a second ago, even though there was no one in there but us. My eyes remained on his face, and while I was scared of my father, I was scared of what was in that other warehouse more.

"They're nobodies, Bastien. Inconsequential. Insignificant. Meaningless."

I wished I could remember her name, but it continued to elude me. We'd never spoken to each other. I wasn't sure if we'd even had a class together. But I somehow recognized her face enough to notice it in a crowded room. "She's not a nobody. I went to school with her. I remember the day she went missing because the entire school had an assembly, and her parents came to talk to us."

My father gave a sigh of irritation and then looked at my brother. "You remember her?"

He shook his head. "I was in lycée at the time."

My father looked at me again. "Are you sure it's her?"

"Yes," I said. "She recognized me. I could tell."

My father returned the papers to the folder before he dragged his hand across his jawline. "Now I understand why you've been so distracted." He got to his feet. "Let's fix that. Come on." He left the warehouse and stepped into the night.

I was quick behind him, hoping that my father would release her so she could go home. She would keep all this a secret in exchange for her freedom. I knew she would. That was a deal I would take in a heartbeat.

We returned to the warehouse with the girls, and my father gestured to his men with the rifles. "Grab her and bring her outside." He pointed out my old classmate then headed back to the door. "Come on, boys."

Godric stayed and exchanged a look with me, and it was the first time he didn't look angry. He was full of resignation, suddenly looking exhausted. Then he gave a slight shake of his head, so slight it was almost unnoticeable. "I fucking told you."

"*Bastien.*"

I followed my father outside. Outdoor lights were flicked on, so the cold ground was visible, covered in patches of white snow. The second I took a breath, ice crystals were in my lungs.

Behind me, the guys escorted the girl outside where we stood. She didn't fight their hold, but they continued to grab her like she was a flight risk. They forced her toward us then pushed on her shoulders so she dropped to her knees, the snow soaking into her jeans.

"Father—"

"No distractions. No compromises. Nothing." He pulled the gun out of the back of his jeans, cocked it, and then forced it into my hand. "If you want to survive in this business then you need to understand everyone is expendable but you and Godric."

I'd never held a gun before, so I held it awkwardly, not wanting to come near the trigger. "What the fuck are you saying?"

"Shoot her."

I took a step back, disturbed by the order he'd just given. "Are you insane?"

"I've never been saner," he said calmly.

"We should let her go."

"Let her go?" he asked incredulously. "So she can run to Mommy and Daddy and tell them what happened here?

Rat us out to the police? The police won't do shit, but our enemies might hit us once they know our location. Everyone is expendable, Bastien."

"Then let her keep working."

"Can't do that either," he said. "Because you're soft—and that's going to change right now."

"I'm soft because I don't want to kill some innocent girl?"

The girl started to cry. Her cries started off small, but as the conversation continued, she began to sob. "Please..."

"Shoot her, Bastien."

"I said I don't want this. I want nothing to do with any of this." I held the gun at my side, and the metal was so cool I could feel it through my gloves. "Give the business to Godric. I want nothing to do with this hell."

My father gave me the coldest stare. "You think you're better than me?"

"That's not what I said."

"I've given you boys everything. The best of everything. And you're gonna stand there and judge me? Little boy thinks he's better than his old man?"

"That's not what I said."

"It fucking sounds like it. My father handed this business to me and my brother, and someday I'll hand it to my two sons. There is no choice in the matter, Bastien. Godric

133

needs someone to watch his back, and you need someone to watch yours."

"I said I don't want it." I said it calmly this time, but I didn't feel the least bit calm. "This is not my path."

Godric shifted his gaze between me and Father.

Father's rage burned in his eyes like bolts of lightning. "Shoot her."

"No."

"Shoot her, or I'll shoot you in the arm. Don't you call my bluff, boy. Because I'll shoot one arm and then the next and then your leg—however many shots it takes for you to be the man you were born to be."

I didn't know what to do, facing off with a version of my father I was better off not knowing. "Does Mother know—"

"She'll be disappointed that her son is a fucking coward."

"And you think it's brave to shoot an unarmed girl?" I exclaimed. "I'm not going to do it."

My father raised his palm to one of his men.

They handed him his pistol.

He cocked it and then aimed it at my arm. "I don't want to do this, Bastien. But mark my words—I will." He held the gun completely steady, aimed at my right arm, finger on the trigger.

"You're gonna shoot me? Your fucking son?"

"Three."

"This is fucking insane!"

"Two."

"Fucking psychopath—"

"One."

I felt the gun lift in my hand and then kick back from the shot.

Bang.

I stumbled backward, the gun still in my hand for a moment before it dropped to the ground. My ears were ringing, the world was spinning, and it took what felt like several seconds to figure out what had happened.

The girl was dead—blood in the snow.

Godric retrieved the gun and stuffed it into the back of his jeans.

My father stood with the gun at his side, but instead of reserving his anger for me, he gave it to Godric with a lethal stare.

Godric held my father's stare in a way I never could. Blue eyes like mine, but with an edge I didn't possess. "I told you he's not made for this."

Chapter 6

Bastien

Five Years Later

I sat by the window, my mind in a haze I couldn't shake. It was summer, one of the warmest days we'd had on record, and I looked out the window at the blue sky and wished it were dark.

My phone rang beside me, and it took me a couple rings to answer it.

Because it was Godric.

I put the phone to my ear. "Yeah?"

"We haven't spoken in two years, and that's what you say to me?"

I continued to look outside, too tired and hungover to really care about much. "Yeah?" I didn't repeat it to be a smartass. Just couldn't think straight right now."

After a long stretch of silence, he spoke. "You're using."

"What the fuck do you want, Godric?" I'd left the house as soon as I was legal and turned my back on my family. But no amount of distance between us could change what I was, could change the crimes of my bloodline, change the fact that I was a Dupont. And no amount of drugs and booze and women could erase the shit I'd seen.

"Dad's dead."

I understood the words perfectly, gave it another moment to soak into my flesh, and I still felt nothing. "Sorry for your loss." I didn't ask what happened because I was sure someone had shot him or tortured him to death. Doubt it was from natural causes.

"Mom is fucked up."

I did feel bad for her. When it came to my father, she looked the other way, but she never did anything herself. I suspected if she'd known what my father had tried to make me do, she would have had a thing or two to say about it.

"She needs us both right now."

She'd tried to get a hold of me over the last couple of years, but I'd always denied her. Didn't want anything to do with another Dupont—even if she was innocent. "She can't have been that surprised."

"I'm gonna come by and get you."

"I'm not going over there."

"It's our mother, asshole."

"She chose to marry him."

"And she chose to have you—don't you forget it."

He was at my apartment thirty minutes later, letting himself inside because I didn't lock the door.

I was still seated at the table, unable to fight the fog in my head.

He came to my side, looked down at me, and then yanked up the sleeves of my shirt.

I twisted out of his grasp and shoved his hand away.

But he saw what he needed to see. He sat down across from me. "Bastien, you're better than this."

"I'm a Dupont. I'm no better than trash."

He sat there, arms across his chest, wearing a t-shirt tight over his biceps. "You're better than this," he repeated. "I know you are."

"You judge me? That's rich."

"I don't judge you. I knew you were having a hard time, but I didn't expect this."

My life had derailed since I'd left the house. I'd turned my back on the family business, but I'd received poor marks in lycée because I was so traumatized by the life my father had exposed me to as a boy. I didn't get into university, so I ended up in the exact place I didn't want to be. But I was a buyer as much as a seller.

"He's gone now. It's over."

"You're in charge now?"

"I guess so."

He was my father's son because he'd been ready for this since the beginning. When he was introduced to the business at the same age I was, he rose to the challenge, was prepared to tackle it head on. "Good luck."

"I've been ready for this for a long time. And I want you to join me."

"Me?" I scoffed. "I'll pass."

"It's what Dad wanted."

"And it's never been what I wanted. Still don't."

"Maybe we can turn over a new leaf."

"I wanted nothing to do with it then, and I want nothing to do with it now."

He gave a slow nod in understanding. "So you can sit around and shoot up all day?"

"Fuck you."

"You're better than this, brother. Way fucking better. Now, get your shit together."

My brother and I had been at odds with each other for a long time, but the message coming from him hit differently than if it had come from somebody else. It was a stab in the lungs, but losing that air forced me to take a new breath. Forced me to confront my image in his eyes. I never thought about my own image, but now I saw it with total clarity. I saw how far I'd fallen, how miserable I'd become, and it hurt like hell.

He slammed his palm on the table as he leaned toward me. "Because you *are* better than this."

We entered my family home, the place I hadn't set foot inside for many years. It was exactly as I remembered, smelled exactly the same, felt like my father still paced in front of the fireplace in his study.

Men were everywhere, instructed to guard my mother from a secondary attack.

We walked into the main sitting room, a round table near the nook off the side of the kitchen. The grand dining table was in a whole different room, could accommodate twenty people for the holidays.

She sat there, her eyes dry from the spent tears and dead inside. A cigarette sat between her fingers, the burning tip dangerously close to her nails. A small pile of ash was underneath her hand, like she'd sat still for minutes and hadn't noticed the cigarette slowly burning away.

I never saw my mother when she didn't look her best. She didn't leave her bedroom unless she was presentable for the day, in her designer clothes and pumps, with her hair and makeup done like she had somewhere to be, even though she usually stayed home all day. It was the first time she'd broken that tradition, her makeup washed away in the flood of tears, her hair knotted like she'd fisted it and tried to yank it out of her scalp. Even at her calmest, she looked deranged.

Godric approached the table first, and even though my mother must have known he was there, she acted like she didn't. The burn of the cigarette continued to inch closer to her exposed skin. "Mother."

She didn't even blink.

He gently took the cigarette from between her fingers and put it out in the ashtray.

She didn't seem to notice.

Godric pulled out the chair to her right and took a seat.

No reaction.

I pulled out the chair across from her and sat down.

Her eyes shifted to me, like she hadn't expected another person, and once the flash of recognition came over her face, her eyes softened into the deepest look of emotion. New tears appeared on the surface of her eyes, my mother's love for me breaking through the mask of sorrow.

I'd turned my back on her the way I had with the rest of my family, even though she hadn't done anything wrong. I just wanted a clean slate, to have no association with the Dupont family at all. But in that moment, I felt like shit about it because it was obvious she truly loved me. My father had viewed Godric and me as pack mules—but not her.

She reached her hand across the table and grabbed mine. "My baby..." She squeezed my hand with both of hers as her bottom lip trembled. She did her best to defeat her emotions and remain strong in a room full of armed guards, but the sight of my face made her succumb to tears.

"I'm sorry, Mom." Sorry that my father was dead. Sorry that I hadn't called.

"I never thought I would be happy again, and then you walked in." She continued to squeeze my hand as she looked at me, her blue eyes identical to mine. Godric was my father's son, but I was my mother's son.

After moments of silence, she finally let me go. She took a breath, let it out slowly, and then cleared her throat. "We'll find out who did this—and we'll make them pay."

I didn't know the details of his death. I assumed their identity was already known.

She turned her gaze on Godric. "You're the head of the family now. You're in charge of the business. I want you to find the motherfucker who took your father from me and bring him to me—so I can shoot him in the goddamn face."

Now I knew why my father had married her.

142

Godric nodded. "Yes, Mother."

She turned to me. "And you will help him, Bastien. You'll watch his back as good as he watches his front. Whoever thought they could hit the Dupont family without consequence was sorely mistaken."

I didn't move an inch, but I felt my body slowly drift away. "I'm sorry that Father is gone, and I hope you find the revenge that you seek. But my stance on the family business hasn't changed. I want no part of it, and no amount of guilt or threat will change that fact. I loved Father in my own complicated, fucked-up way, but I despised what he did."

Godric sat with his arms crossed over his chest, eyes on the table.

My mother stared with her steel-like gaze, clearly unhappy with that answer but maintaining her silence. Father was impulsive with his anger, but Mother was patient. "Godric, give us the room."

Godric rose from the chair. "I have work to do anyway." He left the table, walked toward the armed men, and gestured for them to follow him into the dining room so they could get to work.

Now it was silent, the uncomfortable kind of silent.

"Bastien—"

"Don't waste your time." I didn't raise my voice, not to my mother, but I wanted to. I wanted to shout from the rooftops. No amount of persuasion would change my mind. I thought of that missing girl often, the one shot dead in the snow by my brother's hand. I'd found her name and sent her parents some money anonymously...along with a note saying she was dead. It was cruel, but it was crueler for them to wake up every morning wondering whether she was dead or alive, if she suffered, clinging to a hope that she would ever come back.

"I accept your decision—and I respect it."

My body had tensed in preparation for a fight, but now it relaxed.

"I feel no disappointment, Bastien. Your father was always a madman. I knew that the moment I met him."

"Then why did you marry him?"

Her eyes dropped as she considered the question, and then a painful smile came over her face. "Because I liked that he was a madman." She lifted her eyes again, tears pooled into the corners. "I liked his danger and his wildness. I liked the promise of an extraordinary life rather than an ordinary one. I liked a man who would be a father that would turn my sons into men instead of boys." Her eyes glazed over as she savored the memories of a time before I was even born. It stayed that way for minutes before her gaze sharpened on my face. "You're the same, Bastien. With one major difference—your heart. You've always cared for others as much as you've cared for yourself. Godric was raised in your father's image—a ruthless authoritarian who cares only for himself and his blood. But to you, we're all the same blood. I'm proud of Godric because he's the man we need for this family, but I'm just as proud of you for being greater than this family." She reached for my hand, and she squeezed it again. "You can choose a different path. We can disagree on many things. But no matter what, you will always be a Dupont. You will always be my son."

My hand squeezed hers. "Thank you, Mom."

"I know you and your father had your differences, but he loved you very much."

"Did he?" Because he didn't call me once after I left the house. When I refused to be part of the family business, he said I was a disgrace to the Dupont name. He seemed perfectly content to have Godric as his only son. While I loved him in a very unusual way, I wasn't sad that he was gone.

"Of course."

"I guess I'll have to take your word on that."

"He was a stubborn man. You know this."

"Sounds like an excuse. Because if I were a father, there's nothing that would stop me from having a relationship with my son. And I sure as fuck wouldn't ask him to shoot a girl in his class when he was just fifteen years old. At any fucking age. You were right to call him a madman because only a madman would love his sons based solely on their use."

There was a slight flinch to her eyes, like that assessment offended her.

"Don't tell me my father loved me when all he felt for me was disappointment and then indifference." I pulled my hand away from hers, feeling the surge of anger that had burned in my heart for years. "I'm sorry you lost him. Truly, I am. You don't deserve to suffer like this."

Her eyes remained down on the table.

"I'm sure Godric will make him proud." I sullied the moment with my anger. My mother tried to comfort me with her love, but I pushed her away. My father was long dead, but he continued to haunt every room in which I stood.

"Bastien." She looked at me with pleading eyes.

I should get up and leave, but I stayed. Stayed out of love and respect.

"We don't need to draw a line in the sand. Despite our differences, we're still a family. I want you in this family, Bastien. I want our family dinners on Sunday evenings. I want to call and have you answer. I love you with all my heart."

Guilt struck me like a punch to the face. "I love you too, Mom."

Her eyes crinkled as they softened. "You're still a part of this family, Bastien. You always will be."

We stood in the Père Lachaise Cemetery. It had just started to rain.

We'd picked a matte black casket in which to bury him. The service continued under a sea of black umbrellas, the falling rain the backdrop of sad music. The church had been packed with hundreds of people, but only a few dozen had come to the burial.

People said their goodbyes then left the cemetery, leaving my father to remain in the ground while everyone else carried on with their lives. Godric and I comforted our mother, who sometimes was delirious with sorrow and other times drier than a desert.

The clouds passed, and the rain moved to another spot in Paris. Streaks of sunshine came and went. The waterdrops reflected the light from where they hung on the leaves of the trees and the bushes.

Everyone departed, even my mother, and that left the two of us.

Me and Godric.

Godric hadn't shed a tear. Didn't show an ounce of sorrow —at least publicly. The men who were appointed to guard him kept their distance thirty feet away, creating a perimeter of protection.

Godric stood in a long black coat with gloves on his hands. He lifted his gaze and looked at me.

I stared back.

"You stopped using."

I ignored the statement.

"Good."

It'd only been two weeks, and it had been the hardest two weeks of my life. The only reason I was there that day was by sheer determination. Something about that conversation with my brother had broken the habit. I didn't like the way he'd looked at me, and I didn't like the way I looked at myself.

I didn't want to give him the credit—even if he deserved it. "What's next?"

"Still looking for the asshole who did this. It'll take some time, but I'll find him."

I gave him a long stare. "I'm sure you will, Godric. What about the business?"

"It'll continue uninterrupted. Why fix what isn't broken?"

Every muscle in my body tightened. I saw blood in the snow, smoke from the gun, suppressed rage on my father's ugly face. "Why use trafficked underage women when you can pay for labor?"

He slid his hands into the pockets of his coat as he stood on the other side of Father's grave. He was quiet for a long time, the tension growing between us. "Like Father said, hired help can snitch, prisoners can't."

I shook my head. "You're better than this, Godric."

He smirked slightly when he heard his own words echoed back at him. "That's the difference between us. You are better. I am not."

"It doesn't need to be this way."

"It doesn't," he said. "But it's easier."

"Godric, you and Mom have more money than you even know what to do with. More than you can even wash."

"But if I change the system, and other dealers and enemies find out about it, they'll know I've gone soft. I can't let that happen."

"Someone already killed Dad. You've got a target on your back as we speak. Do the right thing, Godric—"

"If I do, will you come back to the business?"

The question knocked me off my feet because I hadn't seen it coming.

"It's what Dad would have wanted, the two of us together."

"And if I agree, you'll let those girls go?"

"Is that a yes?" He cocked his head slightly.

I wanted nothing to do with the business, even if it was clean. The memory of that night would haunt me for the rest of my life. But I'd accomplished little in my own endeavors, turned to drugs and alcohol like they were the loving arms of someone special. I'd taken my own path and had piss little to show for it. "If we employ hired help, then I'll do it."

Chapter 7

Bastien

Five Years Later

I smoked a cigar in the back seat of the SUV with the window cracked to let the smoke escape and dissipate into the cold winter air. It was a sunny day, a cloudless sky, the sunshine hitting the Eiffel Tower in the most glorious manner.

My phone vibrated in my pocket, and I pulled it out to see the text.

So you're going to ghost me.

It was a girl I'd met last weekend, a friend of a friend of a friend type situation. The chemistry was there like a match to a cigar, and we smoldered and burned. But after the third fuck, I lost interest, like I always did. **I told you it's run its course.** The last time we'd hooked up, I flat-out told her she wouldn't hear from me again—but she texted me anyway.

You're an asshole, you know that?

I was straight with you. If that makes me an asshole, that's fine with me. She was lucky I even bothered to text her back at all. She was just pissed she wasn't getting her way. Thought she was enough to change me, to get me to stick around, but no woman ever made me stick around. *Take care.*

Fuck off, Bastien. The conversation should be over, but the dots were still there like she was typing up a storm.

"Oh boy."

She texted me again. *You think you can treat me like this? Who the fuck do you think you are?*

A ghost. I blocked her.

We pulled up to the house a moment later, and the second I opened the door, I forgot about the woman who'd called me an asshole. I entered the three-story house and headed straight to the dining room, where everyone waited.

When I entered the room, Godric was seated at the head of the table with a drink in his hand, his lit cigar on the ashtray. Everyone else was smoking and drinking, but the air in the room was thick with irritation at my late arrival.

I didn't apologize for the tardiness and dropped into the last open seat.

Godric took a drink before he set it aside. "We all know President Bernard is making things difficult. His strict border control to the north and the south has prohibited the transport of product, and the government sanctions at the port have eviscerated our shipments. We're lucky to ship a fraction of our product. At this rate, all our inventory will expire before we can get it into the hands of buyers, and we'll lose millions."

A new president had been elected, and he had controversial views on international shipments and relations. He wanted to strengthen the French economy by making it a country that produced its own goods rather than relied on our allies for essentials. It wasn't the worst policy I'd ever heard, and I had to give credit where it was due because, unlike French presidents in the past, he was actually getting shit done. But this inadvertently hurt our business. He'd tripled the size of his security checks, and even if we bribed some of them, the number of ships allowed at the port had been reduced to a fraction, so there simply wasn't the same cargo space as before.

And shipments over land were far more likely to get confiscated than by sea.

"So, what do we do?" Godric asked.

The table was full of our partners, people who took our product and sold it through their own channels. Some of them produced their own products as well, but the partnership allowed us to piggyback off one another. They each had their specialties, connections in the Middle East or Eastern Europe, some in Indonesia. It was a global enterprise with its headquarters in the most romantic city on earth.

Herbert was a fat man with a bad toupee and an expensive suit. "Kill him."

I smirked because I assumed it was a joke.

But John, our personal accountant who washed the money and deposited the funds into our various accounts world-wide, seemed to think it was a serious suggestion. "Not a bad idea."

"We can threaten him first," Tony said. "Send a message, and see if that changes his tune."

Godric shook his head. "I can tell he's not that kind of man. Bribery and threats won't work. So, we kill him. Gun him down when he least expects it, the second he steps out of his motorcade. Problem solved."

I looked at my brother and restrained most of what I actually wanted to say. "We are not assassinating a president."

Godric stared at me, and it was obvious he had more he wanted to say too.

The silence stretched and built between us.

Godric finally turned back to our audience. "We'll figure out a solution very soon. Any other issues we need to address?"

John responded. "Profits have dwindled the last nine months. Assumed it was a fluke at first, but as time has gone on, it's clear that it's a trend. I don't believe it's an issue with the product, but the cost."

"I agree," Herbert said. "I voiced this concern long ago." He gave me a look of accusation, knowing full well that I was the one who insisted on paid labor rather than forced labor.

Everyone else at the table gave me the same look, holding me in contempt.

"Correct me if I'm wrong," I said. "Is everyone here a billionaire?" I glanced around the table, looking at everyone, even John.

Of course, no one said a word.

"That's what I thought." I looked at my brother again, expecting him to echo my words.

But he didn't. He said nothing.

"Paid labor stays," I said. "And anyone who disagrees will get a bullet in the back of the head."

Melissa had fallen asleep in my bed.

I wanted her gone, but I wasn't enough of a dick to wake her up just to ask her to leave. I closed the doors that separated the bedroom from the other part of the suite. The space was two thousand square feet on its own and still a fraction of the property.

I sat on the couch, turned on the TV, and lit up a cigar. The only game was a rerun of Manchester United versus

Crystal Palace, a game I'd seen last night, so I flicked through the channels until I found something.

My phone rang in my pocket, and I answered without checking the name of the caller. It was almost eleven in the evening, but it felt like midafternoon. "Yes?"

"Bastien, it's Carl."

"What is it?" Carl was the site manager for our operations. We rotated the location of our production every round so it would be harder to hit us. It drew less attention from anyone in the area too.

There was a pause, far too long for a simple conversation. "There's something you should know, but before I tell you, give me your word Godric will never know it came from me."

The knife of betrayal scraped my skin and was about to draw blood. I gave no audible reaction, grabbed the remote, and turned down the volume so there would be no distractions. "You have my word." And that statement actually meant something because I proved it to my allies as well as my enemies.

"Godric is trafficking again. He's using the girls at another location."

A flashback of that night came back to me, my father aiming his gun at me while he screamed at me to kill some girl whose only crime was being in the wrong place at the wrong time. I still remembered the way the gun shifted in my hand, the way Godric took control and fired the weapon as I still held it. I'd come back to the business under one condition, and he'd revoked that condition without telling me.

"Why increase production if we have no way to sell what we have?"

"I don't know," he said. "But you know Godric better than I do. He's always got a trick up his sleeve."

An old movie played on the screen because there was nothing else to watch, but it was interrupted by sudden news coverage. Two reporters appeared behind a desk on the screen, and the headline below read, "President Bernard Shot."

My mind didn't believe my eyes for a few seconds. All I could do was stare at the screen blankly. "Thank you for the information, Carl." I hung up and turned up the volume on the TV.

The image changed to a reporter on the street, police cars everywhere, along with ambulances. People were crowded on the sidewalk, and the reporter in a heavy coat and gloves spoke. "President Bernard was leaving Sphere when he stepped outside the doors and was shot by a sniper. The president was swiftly taken to the hospital, where he was pronounced dead. There are no leads on the shooter, and no one else was harmed. This is an active investigation, and police have closed off all streets within three square miles. No one can come in or out of the perimeter until they've been thoroughly searched and interrogated..."

I leaned back into the couch as the cigar continued to burn between my fingertips. I hadn't taken a single puff, and now I forgot it even existed—just the way my mother had forgotten her cigarette when my father died.

My father said family was all you could trust.

But now I knew family was who you should trust the least.

The driver let me through the gate to his building. Security didn't search me before I was permitted inside. With my heart pounding in my throat and lava in my veins, I entered his home and waited for the butler to inform him of my arrival.

Of course he was upstairs, probably with a couple whores, since he'd hired someone else to do his dirty work and shoot the fucking president. I looked out the windows to the terrace in the back with the fountain, a slice of privacy in Paris. But no amount of tranquility could calm the rage that had exploded inside my chest.

Godric joined me a moment later. "I think I know why you're here." He was in just his sweatpants, clocked out for the night, relaxing with a bottle of scotch and pussy on his dick. He sauntered toward me with a casual gait, either not concerned by my visit or showing his best poker face.

"I doubt it."

He stopped before me and stared, waited for me to take the first step so he wouldn't have to show his hand.

"I joined the family business under one condition—*one fucking condition*—and you shit all over that." I was angrier than I realized, my voice already bursting like a volcano, screaming at him in his own house.

But he kept his cool, his stare stoic like he wasn't even alive. "I don't know what you're—"

I grabbed him by the throat and punched him so hard in the face his nose broke. Blood dripped all over his face before I shoved him to the floor. "You serious right now? You're going to fucking lie to me?"

He lay there, his hands up like I might try to stomp on his face. The blood dripped over his mouth and chin. With guarded eyes, he watched me, not saying another word.

"I suspected you were going to shoot Bernard, so I tailed you. Followed you to the warehouse on Elm and found those girls there against their will. *Fucking children.*"

He closed his eyes and released a guilty sigh because he'd been caught.

And he had no idea how I'd really gotten the information.

"What the fuck is wrong with you?"

"You heard our partners. They're pissed about the margins, so it was only a matter of time—"

I already knew he'd done it, but to hear him admit it and justify it just pissed me off more. "Fuck you, Godric." I stepped away, knowing I might break his windpipe if I stood there a moment longer.

He got to his feet and wiped the blood on the back of his forearm. "It's an ecosystem, Bastien. If I don't keep all the members of the system happy, it breaks down. They'll come for me, or they'll come for you. If we keep the system happy, then there are no problems. When I said we would do it your way, I meant it. But I have to think about my neck and your neck and Mom's neck. I kept you in the dark to spare you—and that's the honest truth."

I'd made my way toward the window, keeping a huge gap of space between us because I wanted to punch him again.

"I got my hands dirty so yours would be clean."

"And President Bernard? Was that to protect me as well?"

His nose had stopped bleeding for the most part, just trickles coming down. With his arms by his sides, he stared at me in defeat. "It had to be done."

"He was the most popular president we've had in decades."

All he did was shake his head. "It was just going to get harder—"

"There are more important things than money, Godric. Like integrity, which you have none of. President Bernard worked his whole life to reach this moment, and you took it away from him instead of finding a different solution. You didn't even try. Because life and freedom and humanity mean absolute shit to you. You're *him*, for fuck's sake."

"If by him, you mean Dad, then I take that as a compliment."

Divided once again, just as we were when we were teenagers, we were enemies. In the five years we'd worked together we'd grown closer, put aside old resentments, built a relationship that hadn't had a chance to grow. But all of that had gone to piss. "This is the way I see it. I have two choices..."

Some of the blood had dripped over his chin and down his throat. His chest was still because the breaths he took were gentle and even. He appeared calm as he stared at me, but it was all an act.

"I kill you and run the business—since you're incapable of doing it yourself."

He smirked slightly. "You don't have what it takes, Bastien."

"You think so?" I cocked my head as I stared him down. "How long has Dad been dead? Five years now?"

The calm he maintained was suddenly shattered by the question, his eyes narrowed like he didn't understand the direction of the conversation.

"And you've never come close to figuring out who did it. Why do you think that is?"

161

Now, his breathing spiked, his chest rising and falling with the movements of his lungs. He suddenly shifted his weight, his eyes hardening like he saw the monster before him for the first time—and he had no idea I'd been in the shadows.

"Because you never looked in the right place, Godric."

He took a step back, the breath he took so audible, it was like a gasp. In utter disbelief, he had no reaction, no words. He was in shock, so much shock that he couldn't compose himself.

"So, yes, I will fucking do it."

All he did was shake his head slightly, incredulous at the information, refusing to accept it.

"So, should I kill you and run this business ethically? Or will you let the girls go so I don't have to?"

He finally gathered himself. "You kill your own father then act so righteous? Like some kind of fucking savior? Who gives a shit about these girls? They're fucking nobodies—"

"Danielle wasn't a nobody."

He gave me a blank look. "Who the fuck is Danielle?"

"The girl I went to school with. The one you shot."

He shook his head slightly, looking mad as hell. "If only you knew..."

"Only knew what?"

He looked away, his jawline so hard the cords in his neck popped from the strain. "Nothing."

I waited for him to answer me because I couldn't force him to. Even if I put a gun to his head, he was stubborn like our father. "What's your answer?" I pulled the gun out of the back of my jeans and cocked it. "Are those girls going to go free, or are you going to die in the middle of your kitchen?"

Any other time, he would have called my bluff, pressed his forehead right up against the barrel of the gun, between the eyes. But knowing I'd killed our father in cold blood made him realize I was capable of a lot more than he ever knew. "You win, Bastien." He'd looked at me like he hated me so many times, but this look was different. It was lethal. "Congratulations..."

Chapter 8

Bastien

Two Years Later

Paris was alive at all hours of the night, but she was the quietest at four in the morning, when even the night owls couldn't keep their eyes open any longer. The line of SUVs pulled up outside the Louvre, close to the pyramid in the open square. Lights from the lampposts and the buildings were one of the reasons the city had been given its name, City of Light, and it was a name well earned.

The SUV stopped at the curb, and I left the back seat. Snow had fallen the last few days, blanketing Paris in heavy powder. It dusted the statues and sculptures, piled up in the corners of the buildings, away from passersby.

My men formed their perimeter around the perimeter that Godric had already made. Snipers on roofs, men with rifles stationed twenty, fifty, and a hundred feet out. If anyone saw the scene at the iconic establishment, they would assume they had set foot into a war zone.

My boots crunched against the snow as I crossed the empty space to where Godric stood in the light of the pyramid, in his heavy trench coat, a cigar between his lips like he'd made himself comfortable while he waited for me to show up. His hands were in his pockets as he watched me approach.

I wore a long-sleeved black shirt and dark jeans, skipping the jacket because I didn't need that shit. It'd been years since I'd seen him in the flesh. His appearance hadn't changed at all, but mine was nothing like it used to be.

I was always lean, but I'd bulked up over the last few years and covered the track marks with black ink. It turned into a new addiction, and I got one tattoo after the next, turning my body into a tale of death, loss, sorrow—and revenge. I was bigger than my brother, and I knew he wouldn't like that one bit.

I stopped in front of him and looked into the blue eyes that were identical to mine but unfamiliar, like he was a stranger. "Nice coat."

He grabbed his cigar and blew the smoke in my direction, but the wind carried it elsewhere and he missed his mark.

"Did you borrow that from Mom—"

"You think I won't shoot you in the fucking head?" He threw the cigar on the ground and stomped on it.

"I've been shot in the head before." My hand moved to the back of my head, just a couple inches behind my ear, where the hair didn't grow anymore. "Wasn't that bad, honestly."

His eyes shifted back and forth between mine, irritated as hell. "When did you become a smartass?"

"The night I fucked your girlfriend—"

He came at me and swung.

I ducked then blocked his next hit before I kicked him back, and he nearly stumbled ass-first into the snow. It all happened in a matter of seconds.

He gathered himself and did his best to appear unbothered, but it was obvious he wanted to rip my throat out. "Say what you came to say, Bastien."

I did my best to keep the smirk off my face. "I'm sure you've heard the news." Godric had little birds everywhere, people who reported back to him like my birds reported back to me. That was obviously the reason he'd agreed to see me.

His hands returned to his pockets.

"President Martin has appointed me as the First Emperor of the Fifth Republic. That means I run this city. There are no deals that happen without my knowledge. Only through me can distribution take place, can deals be made, can profits soar. I've informed all our previous partners, and they've agreed to work with me directly and cut you out of the deal."

Godric wore his best poker face, but it wasn't good enough.

"If you want to make money, then you work for me too—and you do it by my rules."

"No wonder Dad didn't like you...fucking prick."

I smirked because the insult didn't bother me at all. "He *really* didn't like me when I killed him either."

His confidence wavered, a flicker in his eyes like a candle about to go out in the breeze.

"The old way is gone, Godric. Do business my way—or don't do it at all."

He grounded himself in silence, his viciousness restrained because retaliation would get him nowhere right now. "I thought you were too weak for this life."

"Empathy doesn't make you weak. It makes you honorable, something you would never understand."

He smirked slightly, a forced smile that he clearly didn't feel in his core.

"Anyone who breaks the rules of Fifth Republic will be personally dealt with by me. Violate my rules, and I will treat you no differently than a stranger. Do you understand me?"

He redirected his stare, like he would punch me if he had to look at me for another second. "Fuck off."

"*Do you understand me?*" I grabbed him by the front of the coat and shoved him back. "Because I'm not fucking around. I will turn you into a concrete pillar in one of my skyscrapers. I will chop off your hand and feed it to a stray. I'll make you eat my bullets so you can scream when you shit 'em out." I continued to advance toward him and force him to move back, his men and mine both having their guns trained on one another but unsure whether to fire. "So, I will ask again—do you fucking understand me?"

His eyes were wet, not from emotion, but from angry tears. In that moment more than any other, he wanted me dead. Blood in the snow. Buried in an unmarked grave so no one would remember my name. Piss on the empty gravestone. "Yes, you fucking asshole."

"You only get one chance, Godric." I raised my finger to him. "*One*." Before he could release another insult that would bounce off me like a rubber ball, I turned and walked away. "You better get inside. Wouldn't want you to catch a cold."

Chapter 9

Fleur

When we walked into Holybelly, Luca was already there, in sweatpants and sneakers and a pullover sweater. His expression had been neutral until he realized I was there, and then his look soured noticeably.

Bastien held the door open for me then greeted the waiter, someone he seemed to know well enough to embrace with a hand-grab and a one-armed hug.

I moved to the booth and slid across from Luca. "Morning."

He gave me a nod in acknowledgment and drank from his coffee.

Bastien continued to talk to the waiter, a friendly but heated exchange about the last Manchester United game.

"What are you getting?" I asked as I pulled the menu toward me.

"Food," he said like a smartass.

I should keep my cool to earn his favor, but I'd never been good at that sort of thing. "I'm a lovely person, you know."

"Yeah?" He grabbed the handle of his coffee mug and took another drink.

"What's your problem? You think I'm not good enough for your friend?"

"You dumped him, didn't you?"

I felt betrayed that Bastien had told him, but I knew it was a reasonable thing to share. "I'm sitting here, aren't I?"

He took another drink of his coffee then looked at Bastien, who was still locked in a debate over a game I didn't know he'd watched. He must have left the bed after I'd fallen asleep. Luca gave a sigh then turned back to me. "You want me to be straight with you, sweetheart?"

"You aren't my man, so don't call me that."

He smirked slightly. "In case you haven't noticed, Bastien has put all his chips on you."

I didn't know what I'd done to earn such devotion from a man who could have any woman he wanted. Models and actresses, women ten years younger than me and infinitely more flexible.

"Until I see the same from you, I'm not going to like you."

"Until you stop being a judgmental prick, I'm not going to like you."

Instead of snapping at the insult, his eyes narrowed—and he gave a slight smile.

"I wouldn't be here, stuck looking at your asshole face, if Bastien didn't mean so much to me."

The smirk remained, like my insults were comical rather than threatening. "And how much does he mean to you?"

I shouldn't answer the question, not when I'd only come down here to have breakfast, not face an interrogation. "He means so much to me that I've forsaken all my principles and my fears and my sanity because I can't walk away from him. I'm not ready for a relationship when I'm not even divorced, but I'm in one because I'd rather heal with him than lose him. I'm terrified of his world and the danger in the shadows, but I'm far more afraid of a safe existence without him. You say he's put all his chips in, but he's not the one who has anything to lose. I'm the one betting my life savings. And I'm betting it all because he's the most exceptional man I've ever met. I've known him for such a brief amount of time, but I somehow believe every word out of his mouth, every promise he's ever made to me— even though I've already heard those promises in the past and watched them shatter at my feet."

His smile was long gone, and he just listened, his attention at its highest level.

"And Jesus Christ, he's fucking hot."

He smiled again, but this time, it was genuine, like I'd actually pierced his stone outline and hit him somewhere underneath. He grabbed his mug and took another drink, letting my words slowly dissolve and disappear into the quiet until they were gone.

Bastien finished up with the waiter and slid into the booth next to me. His arm immediately dropped over the back, touching my neck as he picked up the menu that held the specials. "What are you thinking, sweetheart?"

My eyes were still on Luca. "The sweet stack."

"Good choice." He set the menu down and looked at Luca across from him. "You?"

"I'm gonna try the special."

"I'll do the same. Are you going to eat all those pancakes?" He directed the question to me.

"Yes," I said. "Get your own."

When Bastien smirked, he was even more handsome, as if he needed any help in the looks department. "I respect that."

"I do too," Luca said before he took a drink of his coffee.

Bastien seemed to pick up on the tension between us because his eyes shifted back and forth. "I left you alone for two minutes, and you already got into it?"

"Yep," Luca said, his hand still on his mug. "But it was a productive two minutes...because I kinda like her."

Bastien turned his stare on me, affection in his eyes. "Yeah? What did you say?"

"Well, she said I have an asshole face, whatever that means, and called me a judgmental prick."

"That's all true, to be fair," Bastien said.

Luca smirked. "Fuck you, man."

"My woman says how it is," Bastien said with a shrug.

"And everything else she said..." He shifted his stare to me and raised his mug. "We'll keep that between us."

We returned to his apartment after breakfast, and Bastien clearly already had plans for what he wanted to do because he threw me on the bed the second we walked in the door. Instead of asking me to do the things he wanted, he moved on top of me and did all the work, fucking me savagely like it'd been too long since his last release.

Then he just left me on the bed and walked into the bathroom to shower without saying a word.

I listened to the water fall as I lay there for a while, the sunlight coming through the windows because the curtains were parted. The clouds passed, and the light flooded the bedroom for a few moments, bringing a warmth that nearly pulled me into the clouds of dreams.

Penelope Sky

I joined him in the bathroom, a six-foot-something god standing in the shower rubbing a bar of soap all over his body. When the water streaked down the rivers between the muscles of his abs, chest, and arms, it shone, making his muscled mass more distinct. His ink glistened too, and I was reminded just how hot he was...like I'd somehow forgotten.

His eyes moved to me through the glass as he continued to wash himself. "Come on." He nodded for me to join him behind the glass, a shower with two showerheads.

I undressed and left my clothes on the counter around the bathtub then joined him under the water. My eyes closed as I tilted my head back and let the warmth stream down my body.

His soapy hands gripped my tits and massaged them with the soap, his chin down and his eyes soaking in the curves of my body like he hadn't just taken me roughly as soon as we'd walked in the door from breakfast.

How did he desire me so deeply when he could replace me with someone younger? A woman who was a zero or even a double-zero. I wanted to voice my curiosity, but I was afraid that I would plant the idea in his head and this erotic fairy tale would be over.

His eyes lifted to mine, like he'd somehow felt my change in mood. "What is it?"

"How do you do that?"

He smirked like he knew exactly what I was referring to. "Quick reflexes won't keep you alive, not when you have to react to something without notice. It's intuition that saves your skin, detecting the threat before it's fully formed. And I know you well enough now to feel your changes in mood as they happen. So, what is it?"

"I'd rather not say."

"You want me to be honest with you? Then be honest with me." He didn't say it with a tone of anger, just a calm simplicity.

My eyes dropped to his wet chest, the fair skin obscured by dark ink, a man who was covered in layers of muscles. "Sometimes I don't understand your fascination with me, is all."

"Really?" He gave me a quick look-over, tits to pussy.

"Well, you could have a woman ten years younger, and her tits would be even better."

He cocked his head slightly, and his eyes narrowed just a smidge, like he was truly surprised by that response. "I remember who I was at twenty-three. I had to grow up fast, but even then, I was still a child in many ways."

"I don't see why that matters."

"Because a twenty-three-year-old woman is too young for me."

"To fuck?" I asked incredulously.

His eyes narrowed farther. "You think all we're doing is fucking? I made it clear—"

"This is why I didn't want to say anything."

He seemed on the verge of getting angry, but he swallowed it back and kept the calm. "Help me understand."

"Look at you." I gestured from his shoulders to his fat dick between his legs. "You could have anyone, have as many girls as you want at once, and you're choosing to spend your time with me, a woman about to be divorced and almost thirty. It just seems a little unbelievable sometimes."

He stared at me long and hard, the sound of the falling water fading out in the tension. "You're crazy, you know that?"

"I'm not crazy—"

"You're fucking crazy. Crazy to let that asshole steal your confidence. Crazy to let that idiot strip you down to a hollow shell of insecurity. Let me tell you something about men, sweetheart. They cheat because they cheat. It's as simple as that. His gaze didn't wander because you were less than, because your ass wasn't hard enough or your tits weren't perky enough."

"I appreciate that, but that has nothing to do with it."

"It has everything to do with it. Because there's no fucking way that a woman who looks like you could possibly question her worthiness otherwise. Why would I want a woman ten years younger than me when I can have you? A woman who's intelligent, experienced, speaks her mind, whose sass hits harder than a goddamn bullet." He grabbed me by the throat like he was about to slam me to the floor. "You're. Fucking. Crazy." He squeezed me before he let go. He turned off the shower then stepped out, pulling the towel off the rack and drying himself quickly.

I followed him and stood on the bath mat, soaking wet because I didn't have a towel.

He tossed me his when he was finished.

"Look, I just mean—"

He turned back to me, sexy with his damp hair a mess from the towel. "I thought we were done with this."

"I just think someone like you would be one of those guys who never wants to commit or settle down because you don't have to."

His furious eyes stared into mine like I offended him.

"That's all I'm saying."

"You're right. That's exactly who I was." His eyes remained on mine, still furious and hard in intensity, like he was about to snap and scream at me. The silence trickled between us, but instead of letting the intensity disperse, it only got worse. I saw a slight tremor in his body, a tightness in his neck that nearly snapped the cords under the skin. "Until I met you."

A wave of raw emotion swept through me, a combination of so many different feelings that I couldn't tell them apart. I was touched by the words and the affection packed behind them—and I was fucking scared.

"You asked me, sweetheart."

"I said I'd rather not say, and you pushed."

"You want honesty, and that's a two-way street."

"I know what I said—"

"Ask me how I feel about you."

"Bastien, this is going way too fast—"

"It's going exactly the pace it's supposed to," he said. "Now, ask me."

I knew what he would say, and while those words would bring me unimaginable joy, they would also bring a vulnerability I couldn't handle right now. I was becoming thinner, weaker, and more transparent by the day—and infinitely more fragile.

When he knew I wasn't ready, he turned away and walked out of the bathroom.

Once I was alone, my breaths grew deep and labored, the danger gone but the fear profound. I waited a minute or two before I stepped into the bedroom, seeing him dressed in only his sweatpants. Sunlight continued to come through the open curtains and highlight the elegant bedroom fit for a ruler.

He stepped into the other room, probably to sit on the couch and watch TV.

I didn't know if I should get dressed and leave...or stay. He seemed to have shut me out, so I wasn't sure. Instead of getting dressed and making assumptions that might piss him off, I approached him on the couch. "Should I go?"

He didn't look away from the TV, which was on now. His muscular back was to me, the dark ink a distinct contrast against his fair skin. His body was still, like it didn't draw breath the way mine did. "I never want you to go, and you know that."

***

The weekend came and went, and I was back to the daily grind of a regular person. Being at my desk before nine, eating my lunch by myself, walking home at five, sometimes in the rain.

It was tense between Bastien and me after that fight, if you could call it a fight. That seemed to be the number one cause of strife in our relationship, him wanting to hit the gas while I wanted to hit the brake.

But I *didn't* want to hit the brake. I just didn't want to go a hundred miles an hour.

However, Bastien had been in the driver's seat from the beginning—and he wouldn't give up the wheel.

It'd been a couple days since I'd seen him. I'd spent the entire weekend at his house, so I didn't expect a sleepover for a while. He probably had work that needed his attention, details he didn't share with me because I'd rather not know. But he texted me every day, several times a day. For a man who's never been a boyfriend, he knew exactly how to do it. When we were apart, I didn't worry about what he did behind my back. He must get offers left and right, but I wasn't scared he would cash one of them in. Maybe it was because I trusted him without even realizing it.

When I got off work on Wednesday, I texted Adrien. ***Can I come by?***

His dots were immediate, something that hadn't happened during our marriage. Hours would pass before I'd get a response from him. I didn't think anything of it at the time. I wasn't needy and insecure—not like I was now.

Another thing I liked about Bastien. I never had to be needy and desperate for his attention or validation because he gave it before I had to ask. He let me know every day that I was the one woman on his mind. He was always available for my texts and calls, anytime—day or night.

I appreciated it more than words could say.

Yes, I'm home.

Okay, be there in ten.

I'm excited to see you.

I rolled my eyes before I pocketed the phone.

Ten minutes later, I arrived at the house that used to be mine, the smell exactly as I remembered, everything feeling familiar and foreign at the same time. Our wedding picture used to be on the wall in the entryway, but I noticed it was missing.

Adrien joined me a moment later, his eyes lit up like stars at the sight of me. He went straight for me, opening his arms to hug me.

I stepped back. "What the fuck are you doing?"

He stilled, all his joy quickly erased by confusion. "I—I'm sorry." He took a few steps back, his mood noticeably souring when he didn't get what he wanted.

I looked at the wall where the picture had been, its absence noticeable because of the empty space. "Looks like I'm not the only one ready for a new chapter."

His eyes followed mine. "It's not what it looks like. It fell and broke. I'm getting it reframed."

"It just fell?" I asked skeptically. "An invisible earthquake came through?"

He sighed. "I didn't take it down, Fleur. But I would be lying if I said I wasn't pleased that you're offended by the thought of me taking it down. That means there's still something here."

"You misunderstand me. If you're taking down our wedding photo to hide it from the women you invite over but you won't give me a divorce, that pisses me the fuck off. Don't make me jump through hoops, Adrien."

"That's not what's happening."

"Whatever. It doesn't matter." I wasn't going to argue with a liar. "I need that divorce."

"Our next mediation is in three weeks—"

"I want it now," I demanded. "No more games. No more procrastination. Just give me the fucking divorce."

He watched me for a while, a blanket of fear masking his face. He swallowed before he spoke. "What's the rush?"

"That's my business."

"Are you going to marry this guy or something?"

"Adrien, we aren't getting back together. Do you understand that? Because I don't think you do."

He continued his stare, looking dead behind the eyes. "I told you he's not good for you."

"You were supposed to be, and look how that turned out," I snapped. "Whether Bastien is in my life or not, I'm never going back to you. So stop with the games, and let's just finish this."

"What's the rush?" he repeated.

"I said it's none of your business."

Despite his best efforts to appear calm, he lost his footing. "Did he ask you to marry him?"

"Adrien."

"Answer me."

"I've gone into this relationship with Bastien with restraint, and I don't want to feel restrained anymore. I don't want to be married anymore. I want to be divorced, I want to put this behind me, and I want to be fully invested in my new relationship. But that's hard to do when I know I'm technically married to you."

"It's hard because you still feel something for me."

"Trust me, that's not the case," I insisted. "I want to close this chapter in my life and open a new one with Bastien. The relationship is new and I'm in no hurry to rush to the finish line, but I want to be ready for when that moment comes."

All he could do was stare at me, his deepened breaths visible as the discomfort took hold. He looked more forlorn than when I moved out, when he'd told me there had been more women than Cecilia. He knew he was about to lose me for good, and there was nothing he could do to stop it. "Fleur, I don't want to lose you."

Maybe I was crazy, but in that moment, I actually pitied him. "Adrien, I know it's hard to let go, but I'm already gone. Even if I wanted to forgive you and work on the relationship, I can't."

"Why?" he whispered.

I thought the reason was obvious. "Because I'm in love with someone else." They were words I couldn't even admit to myself, and no way in hell could I ever say them to Bastien, not when he would swallow me whole. But I could say them to Adrien because...he needed to hear them. He needed this truth, no matter how painful, for closure.

He clenched his eyes shut like that would somehow block out the sound of my words. His face was already pale when it was normally tanned, but now he looked on the verge of being sick. It reminded me of the way I'd looked when Cecilia told me about his infidelity, how I'd looked every day for a month when I lived in that small apartment and cried myself to sleep every night. This moment should taste like vindictive revenge, but it was so bland I couldn't taste it. The last thing I wanted was to inflict that kind of pain on anyone, even him.

It gave me no pleasure, none at all.

He finally opened his eyes again. They were slightly wet from the tears he tried so hard not to shed in front of me. "I'll do it." He spoke so quietly, his words were barely audible. "Whatever terms you want, I'll give them to you."

"Thank you, Adrien." The defeat meant the world to me, the war finally over. I'd left this house almost four months ago, and when I'd walked out with my bags, I assumed I would be miserable for a very long time. I assumed it would take years to put myself back together, and by then, the dating pool would be empty and I would die alone. Never did I expect the most remarkable man to walk into that bar and change the colors of my life from black-and-white to glorious Technicolor.

I opened my arms and hugged him tightly, and for the first time, I felt only love for him. I let my anger and resentment dissolve in the air around us. I let the past remain in the rearview mirror. Instead of eviscerating him with the talons of my heartbreak, I chose to comfort him as a friend.

He squeezed me hard and rested his chin on my head, giving a heavy breath that was full of both joy and pain. "I love you, Fleur. Always will."

———

I'd just gotten home from work after buying a baguette at the bakery. I had an assortment of cheeses that I'd picked up a few days ago from Le Grande Épicerie and they were still good, so I made a snack in my little kitchen, smearing the cheese on the edge of the bread before I took a bite. I was still in my heels and my coat, the raindrops glued to the windows of my apartment. I leaned against the counter, mentally drained from staring at the computer screen and doing spreadsheets and booking appointments. The work was boring and unfulfilling, but it was good pay. Now I had the heater where I wanted it, could get groceries delivered instead of using what little time I had left to take care of that myself. Money didn't buy happiness, but it bought time, and that freedom was happiness.

My phone vibrated in my pocket. It was Bastien. **What's my woman doing?**

Standing in my kitchen eating cheese and a baguette. What about you?

Just took care of something.

That could mean anything. Killing someone or signing paperwork. I'd rather not know which.

Put down that baguette and have dinner with me.

It's a really good baguette...but you're really hot...what will I choose?

He didn't say anything. His dots didn't appear.

Looks like the sexy man wins.

Good choice, sweetheart. I'll be there in five minutes.

I left my apartment and exited the lobby to the street. Bastien was already there, wearing a long-sleeved shirt with the sleeves pushed to his elbows. He was dressed in dark colors, a dark blue shirt with black jeans. A grin slid over his face at the sight of me, and he moved into me and kissed me right there on the sidewalk, gripping my ass through my skirt. He abruptly pulled away and opened the back door for me to get inside.

The driver took us a few blocks away before he pulled up outside an expansive restaurant. There was a sea of tables covered in white tablecloths with little white vases on top, each holding a single white rose. Bastien pulled out the chair for me then took the seat across from me.

He grabbed the menu and took a look, distracted for a second so I could stare at him.

My god, he was so good-looking. Soft eyes in a hard face with a sharp jawline. He always carried himself with the kind of confidence that commanded the room. Even when he was seated, he felt like the tallest person in the restaurant.

His eyes flicked up to me, like he felt my stare.

I tried to hide how obvious I was. "Let me guess...you're getting the steak."

He smirked at the comment and placed the menu aside. "Roast chicken. Need to cut back on the red meat."

"And the cigars...and the scotch." I smiled so he knew I was teasing.

Playfulness was in his eyes. "I'll give up red meat before I'd give up either of those things."

"Really? I figured you would give up the cigars first."

"No. Speaking of cigars, I noticed you haven't smoked in a while."

"You're right, and I didn't even notice." The separation from Adrien stressed me out, but life had become easier since. Didn't even realize I didn't need it anymore. Bastien had taken up my entire focus. I looked at the menu. "I don't know what to get."

"Full of that baguette?" he teased.

"No. Everything just sounds so good." I continued to stare at the menu. "Do I want the pasta or the pizza? Sometimes life can be so hard."

He smirked. "Get both."

"I can't eat both, and I'm not sure if I'm offended or pleased that you think I can." I set the menu aside.

"Take one to work tomorrow."

"I already sit on my ass all day. I can't sit there and eat pasta."

"You can sit on my face all day if you want."

I smiled at the joke.

But he stared at me like it wasn't a joke at all.

The waitress came over, and the second she got a full view of Bastien, she hesitated before she spoke, like she was blind-sided by a man so good-looking. Her eyes were wider than they should be, and she fumbled for her pad in her apron.

I couldn't be angry, not when I understood all too well.

"What can I get you?" she finally said.

"We'll take a bottle of the Bordeaux," Bastien said. "I'll take the chicken, and she'll have the margherita pizza and the baked ziti."

Did he really just order both for me?

"Of course." She took the menus and left.

"How did you know I wanted the margherita pizza?" I asked.

"Because you seemed to like it when Gerard made it for you."

He paid that much attention? That was something Adrien never would have remembered. "Our waitress must be judging me right now."

"Who cares if she is."

Probably wondering what a man like him was doing with a girl who ordered two entrees.

She came back a moment later, uncorked the wine, and filled his glass first, and when he gave a nod, she poured the rest and walked away.

The restaurant was only half full, quiet because it was early for the dinner rush. Bastien and I normally had dinner much later in the evening, but now that I had a job that required me to be behind the desk by nine every day, that had changed.

He drank his wine, licked his lips, and then relaxed in the wooden armchair, his arm over the back of the chair beside him.

I was perfectly content sitting in silence, enjoying the sight of this beautiful man across from me. Beautiful wasn't even the right word, because a rose in a garden could be beautiful, and this man was hard as stone and rugged as a tree trunk.

He held my stare like he was even more comfortable with the silence, could sit in it for hours.

"How was your week?" I asked.

After a long pause, he gave a slight shrug. "Same as always."

"What do you do, exactly?"

"On the first of the month, tariffs are due. The weeks leading up to that are spent policing production and distribution, having unscheduled pop-ins to keep everyone on their toes. There are meetings with dealers and investors. And then my obligations to the Senate and President Martin."

"You sound so busy, I don't know how you have time for me."

"I don't have time for you," he said. "I *make* time for you."

I looked into those confident eyes and felt myself float.

"You're my priority, and it's my job to make you feel like a priority."

"You know, for a man who's never been in a relationship, you're awfully good at it."

He gave a slight smirk. "Because there's only one relationship I've ever wanted to be in."

The fact that he'd chosen me of all people still shocked me, but I didn't voice that insecurity when it would only ignite his fury.

He drank his wine again.

"Do you mind if I ask you questions about work?"

"No."

"You said you used to be a hit man?"

"For a brief time."

"So, people would just pay you to kill someone?"

"More complicated than that," he said. "I didn't aimlessly kill anyone. The target had to deserve it. So, men would hire me to take out the enemies they couldn't take out on their own. If the target was ever a woman, I would kill the man who hired me instead. And if a woman hired me, I'd do it for free."

"Why would a man want to kill a woman?"

"The number one reason is because she's a mistress. She

threatened to tell his wife, so instead of paying her to be quiet, he'd rather pay me to kill her."

I gave a slow nod in understanding. "A whole different world out there..."

"That world is your world—but you don't see it."

I was glad I didn't see it. "You said you did that for a brief time. What else did you do?"

"The drug business. I grew up in it, and I'll die in it."

"What do you mean you grew up in it?"

He was quiet for a while before he answered. "It was the family business. When I was fifteen, I was forced into it."

I cocked my head as I listened to that answer. "Your mother ran a drug empire?"

"My father."

I remembered one of our first conversations where he gave me conflicting information. "You said you never knew your father."

"And I didn't." His mood soured noticeably, like speaking of him was a sore subject, like there was an entire wall of secrecy behind it. "We never got along. From the moment I was born to the moment he died, we were at odds with each other. We had very different business philosophies."

He didn't raise his voice or deepen his tone, but I could tell by the look on his face that this was a serious point of contention. There was an injury underneath the surface that hadn't healed, and the wound continued to fester as time passed. Something told me I shouldn't pry into this territory. It was like when I'd asked him why he felt so protective of the girls who were forced into hard labor. Bastien was easygoing and calm, like he didn't carry the burdens the rest of us did, but it was clear that wasn't the case. "So, this is the only life you've ever known."

He stared at me for a while before he agreed. "You could say that."

"Is this the only life you've ever wanted?"

He was quiet again, a pause so long, it seemed like he wouldn't provide an answer to follow it. "There was a time when I wanted something else. To take a path no one else in my family wanted to walk. But I learned the hard way that this is what I'm destined for. I'm a criminal who earns his living in unsavory ways, but innocent lives remain untouched because of it, so some good comes from it."

I wanted to ask how many people he'd killed, but I chose to keep the question to myself. I appreciated what he shared with me, especially since it visibly pained him to do so. "You're so wealthy, I'm sure you could retire whenever you wanted."

"Yes, but it's not about the money."

"Then that means you enjoy it."

"I'd be lying if I said I didn't," he said. "When I left my father's house, I wanted to do something more with my life. But it was too late. I'd already made too many mistakes, and I got into drugs instead."

The intense conversation dropped when the waitress brought our entrees—all three of them.

I looked at the pasta and then the pizza, and I didn't know which one looked better.

Bastien looked at me with a sly smirk before he dropped his linen across his lap. His elbows moved to the table, and he started to feast on his roast chicken, a man who had to eat thousands of calories a day to keep up all the muscle on the steel of his bones. Sometimes he would look at me, but most of his attention was on his food, like a hungry bear.

I went back and forth between the pasta and the pizza, even scooping the pasta onto a slice and trying it that way. My food was a lot better than his, all fat and carbs, while he stuck to his chicken, rice, and veggies. But that was why he was hot and I had an ass.

He stopped eating, and his eyes were on the door, lingering there for a long time with a blank expression on his face.

Half of his food was still on the plate, and I'd never seen him not finish a meal, so I asked, "Did you not like the food?"

He didn't blink. Kept up the hard stare like he saw someone he recognized but didn't want to see.

I started to turn to look over my shoulder.

"Don't move." His voice was quiet, and his words were quick.

The relaxed ambiance between us suddenly disappeared when I detected the warning in the air. When I felt the hostility pour off him in waves. It seemed like my heart had stopped because I took his words so literally.

He continued his hard stare, not blinking once.

"Should I be worried—"

"Get down."

"What—"

He didn't ask me again. He got to his feet and flipped the table, our food falling to the floor and the plates shattering. He pushed me down to the floor and shoved the table up against the wall, putting me in a cage without a roof.

I let out a little scream when I hit the floor because someone came at Bastien from behind, brandishing a long knife.

Bastien executed a series of moves that happened so fast, throwing up his elbow to hit the assailant in the face before he grabbed the guy's arm and spun it down, slamming the blade into his thigh.

The guy screamed, the knife impaling him.

Bastien punched him hard before he yanked the knife out by the hilt and threw him aside.

I saw the guy hit the floor, screaming in anguish as he gripped his thigh and he tried to stop the bleeding.

Then I heard gunshots.

"Oh my god..." I stayed there, staring at the man bleeding to death on the floor, terrified the same would happen to me but with bullets instead of knives.

I could hear the commotion, hear the sounds of grunts and yells as the fighting continued. I knew Bastien was alive because there would be no fight if he were dead. Desperate to see what was happening, I inched closer to the man who continued to scream, and I peered around the corner.

Bastien made a flurry of moves that looked like action stunts in a movie from Hollywood, successfully spinning the gun out of his enemy's hand and then firing at the next guy who came at him with a knife. It was three on one, but Bastien managed to hold his own, kicking ass in a fight he hadn't known was coming.

He slammed one guy's head onto the edge of the table, and his neck cracked when it broke. He was dead on the floor, eyes wide and lifeless.

The guy screaming next to me looked at me, but he seemed to be too distressed to come for me.

Bastien grabbed the next guy then literally threw him, sending him crashing into another table.

The last one hesitated before he faced off with Bastien, like he knew he was in deep shit.

Bastien tossed the gun aside like he preferred hand-to-hand combat rather than a cheap shot. He came at him in a rush, throwing a fist hard into his face before pummeling him again, moving at a speed that seemed impossible with his large mass.

The guests in the restaurant had already run out. The waiters had ditched too. Police had probably been called and were rushing to the scene, but by the time they got there, the fight would already be over.

Bastien grabbed the guy by the throat and slammed him down into the floor like he weighed nothing. Then he loomed over him like an intimidating statue about to come to life. He lifted his heavy boot and propped it against the front of the man's neck, but he kept his weight on his back foot.

The guy lay still, his chest rising and falling with his deep, labored breaths.

Bastien stared down at him. "Tell me who sent you, or I'll break your windpipe."

I should duck behind the table again because I didn't want to see this. Didn't want to watch Bastien make good on his threat right in front of me. But my eyes stayed in place, needing to see the outcome of the attack. The guy beside me had started to bleed out and went silent. He continued to breathe because he was still alive, but not for long.

The man under Bastien's foot kept his silence.

"And you know breaking your windpipe is only the beginning."

He trembled on the floor, straining to draw breath as Bastien applied more pressure with his foot. "Based on the pathetic way you guys came at me, he sounds like an amateur. Are you willing to die for an amateur?"

Once Bastien applied more pressure, he tried to grab Bastien's shoe and push back, but since Bastien had to weigh over two hundred pounds in muscle, it was point-less. "Please... If I tell you, he'll kill my family."

Bastien kept his foot in place with a stonelike expression. "Then this is your fault for working for a man who has no honor. And you deserve what's about to happen to you."

"You could let me go—"

Without warning, he struck like a viper and slammed his foot down on the man's throat.

I looked away so I wouldn't have to see it.

There was no scream, not when his throat collapsed. The sound he made was like a guttural moan.

Then I heard Bastien stomp again, and that made the man wince like an animal that had been shot but forced to live. There was another stomp and a restrained scream—and then silence.

I squeezed my eyes closed even though I was behind the table and gripped my arms with clenched hands, shaking like I was the bleeding victim instead of some man who had just tried to kill us. My knees were to my chest, and somehow, the silence was more painful than the noise.

Then Bastien spoke to someone he knew, like he was on the phone. "Must be doing a good job...because some assholes just tried to kill me."

———

Bastien pulled the table away like I was trapped against the wall and couldn't get out.

I just chose to stay there and hide.

"Sweetheart." He kneeled down beside me, blocking my view of the guy who'd bled out.

It took several seconds for me to have the courage to look him in the eye.

His stare was no longer vicious like it'd been during the fight. It was kind and gentle, the way it was whenever he comforted me. His blue eyes shifted back and forth between mine as he assessed my state of mind. "I'm sorry you had to see that."

I trembled like I was afraid of him, but I just needed more time to process what had happened. "Me too."

"It's over now."

I nodded, even though I wasn't sure why.

He continued to assess me. "You're still afraid. I hope I'm not the one you're afraid of."

I wasn't afraid of him, but only because we were allies and not enemies. However, under different circumstances, I would be utterly fucking terrified. "No, of course not. I'm —I'm just overwhelmed."

"Come here." He was on one knee, and he opened his arms to take me.

I left the wall and moved into his chest, and then I felt his thick arms encircle me and hold me close. They were the same arms that had destroyed all his opponents, but they made me feel safer than I ever had.

"It's okay." He rested his chin on my head as he held me tight. "I'd never let anything happen to you, sweetheart." He dipped his mouth and pressed a kiss to my hair as he cocooned me in the safety of his arms.

"Bastien."

I didn't know Luca very well, but I recognized his voice.

Bastien let me go and rose to his feet.

Luca was accompanied by other men, all dressed in black. He looked around at the scene as he walked up to his friend. The police hadn't shown up yet. "How'd they know you were here?"

I stayed on the floor because I wanted to disappear into the corner.

"They must have been tailing me. The only people who knew about my dinner plans were Fleur and my driver."

"And you trust your driver?" Luca asked.

"Yes."

Luca didn't ask if he trusted me. His eyes found mine across the room. Even though he spoke loud enough for me to hear, he talked about me like I was deaf. "She okay?"

"Shaken up, but she'll bounce back."

"Or she'll bounce out..."

Bastien ignored what he said and nodded toward the man he'd killed with just his boot. "Wouldn't talk. Said his employer would kill his family."

"Think it was Godric?"

Bastien didn't hesitate before he answered. "No."

"Why are you so sure?"

"Because if he wanted me dead, he'd want me to know."

Luca nodded to one of his men. "Load 'em up." He turned back to Bastien. "Called off the police. Tried to keep it from the press, but I was too late. Martin will be pissed about the backlash."

"I can't control the people who want to kill me."

"It's literally your job, Bastien."

Bastien watched the men remove the bodies and clean up the mess left behind. "No one has put a hit on me in a long time. So, they are either very stupid—or very desperate."

"Maybe they're angry with how we handled Regis."

"We handled Regis how we handle everyone else."

"Oscar?"

Bastien shook his head. "He has other interests right now."

Luca stood there with his arms across his chest. "When you're at the top, all eyes are on you. Perhaps someone else wants to be seen."

"I'd be more concerned if this weren't the most amateur attack I've ever seen."

"Maybe that was why they did it," Luca said. "Because you wouldn't have suspected it..."

Bastien dropped me off at home.

He had business that required his attention, had to shake down his contacts to figure out who wanted him dead, so he didn't have time for me. I got a quick kiss and a pat on the ass as a goodbye.

I didn't want him to leave, but I didn't want to ask him to stay—so I let him go. Despite the fact that I was unnerved by what happened, I wasn't his priority right now. He had an entire city to run.

I went to work the next day and the next, the office exactly the same as usual, like whatever had happened the other night hadn't affected this sector of his business. The attack at the restaurant was on the news, but reporters were calling it a failed robbery attempt.

I knew what had really happened.

I slept like shit every night, having nightmares about the violence I'd witnessed. I didn't care about the welfare of the man with a stab wound in his leg beside me, but I wondered if he'd survived. Or maybe he did survive, and then Bastien killed him.

I knew Bastien was really wrapped up in the chaos when he didn't text me. It was the first time in our relationship that I felt his absence when I needed him more. But out of fear of seeming clingy or desperate, I let it be.

Chapter 10

Bastien

I entered my mother's house and was escorted to the drawing room. Like she was a queen and I was a peasant, I waited for her to join me.

Nearly twenty minutes later, she graced me with her presence, fully done up like she expected a male suitor. Luminous pearls hung around her neck, and she wore a gray and black ensemble, like she was ready to go out rather than spend the evening at home.

"I hope I'm not interrupting your plans for the evening."

"You're never an interruption, dear." She came to me, and I had to bend my knees so she could kiss me on each cheek. "Would you like to join me for dinner?"

I was too busy to sit down for a meal. Had been too busy even to see my girl. "I need to speak with Godric."

Her eyes glazed over with disappointment. "I helped you once. I won't do it again."

"It's important—"

"It's always important."

"I just need his number."

"Your brother is already not speaking to me. I know in time he'll come around because I'm stuck between a rock and a hard place with you two. But if I give this to you, it'll take even longer for him to come back to me."

"He doesn't need to know you gave it to me, Mom."

Her hands came together at her tight waist, her nails done in French tips. "Don't put me in the middle."

"I'm not—"

"You are. All I want is to be a mother to my two sons, not be a soldier on the battlefield, fighting in a war I don't support. What I want is for the two of you to reconcile, to put aside your differences and be brothers—"

"We weren't brothers when we were kids, we aren't brothers now, and we'll never be brothers." I didn't mean to be harsh, but I needed my mother to understand that her wish was hopeless. "I'm sorry."

"I don't understand."

"The details don't matter." He betrayed me and I betrayed him. Simple as that.

She continued to stare into my eyes with a slight plea. "I won't help you, Bastien."

"I have no intention of harming him. I just need to speak to him."

"With your grand shadow across this city, I'm surprised you don't have the resources to find what you seek on your own."

It was far more complicated than she realized. "If I pursue him myself, one of us will end up dead. Out of respect for you, I've kept my distance so I won't kill him and he won't kill me. If you want it to stay that way, then you'll give me his number."

She gave a sigh as she looked away, frustrated that she was in the middle once again. "When we had Godric, your father was satisfied he'd gotten his son and had no desire for more children. I insisted on another because I didn't want Godric to be alone when we were gone. But it looks like that's going to happen anyway."

My father never showed love to either one of us. We'd always been workers in his anthill. We had one purpose, to continue the family business under the Dupont name, like it was some kind of fucking legacy. "I won't tell him you were the source."

"Then what will you say?"

"Trust me, he won't ask." Any respectable man wouldn't ask for his enemy's playbook. Too much pride. Too much

206

stubbornness. And Godric had a healthy dose of both those things.

"You already spoke to him, Bastien. What else needs to be said?"

"That's my business." I wouldn't rattle my mother by telling her someone had put a hit on me. That someone could be out for revenge or someone wanted to remove me from power and take my place. Right now, I didn't know, and none of my contacts seemed to know either. Godric wasn't part of my world, so he might know something. "Mom."

She looked away again, the frustration bubbling in her eyes. "Fine."

I sat in the back seat parked at the curb, raindrops breaking their contact with the window and streaking down. The phone was to my ear, and I listened to it ring a few times before my brother answered. "Yes?"

"It's Bastien."

There was a pause—but that pause said so much.

"I'm sure you heard what happened the other day."

He said nothing, either confirming that fact or pretending otherwise.

"You said people wanted me dead. Looks like you were right."

"What do you want from me, Bastien?"

"Tell me who—because you obviously know who it is."

He was quiet for a long time, probably sitting at home in one of his many apartments. He owned a vast portfolio of real estate in Paris, so it was hard to know where he was at any given time. "I warned you to walk away."

"You know I don't walk away from anything."

"Then there's nothing else to discuss."

I hadn't expected to get much out of him, but I'd expected more substance than this. "You'd have to be pretty heartless to look the other way while someone tries to kill your only brother."

He gave a quiet chuckle. "Not as heartless as killing my own father."

The insult rushed right past me, and I felt no remorse.

Godric said nothing else.

A thought had been at the back of my mind for a long time, for years, but I'd never had the opportunity to ask for answers. "Why haven't you told Mom?" I had no doubt she didn't have any idea, because if she knew, she'd never speak to me again.

He didn't say anything.

"Why?" I pressed. "She'd turn her back on me if she knew. That's exactly what you'd want, right?"

He remained quiet.

I waited for him to explain.

"Because it would kill her, Bastien. Don't think for a fucking second that I'm protecting you. I'm protecting her —because she'd swallow a bunch of sleeping pills and never wake up if she knew it was you."

I let his words bite into me with sharp fangs. I felt no guilt for my actions, but I felt like shit for what I'd done to my mother. I'd made her a widow decades sooner than she needed to be. "It doesn't have to be this way, Godric."

"If you're going to tell us how to do business, then yes, it needs to be this way."

"You make it sound like you're the one gunning for me."

It was dead quiet wherever he was, so he must be at home, probably in front of the fire, a sleeping woman in his bed. There was no sound of his breath, like a cigar was squeezed between his lips and teeth. "I'm not. But I know who is—and I'm not going to stand in his way."

I miss you, sweetheart. It'd been a few days since I'd spoken to her. I'd been so absorbed in tracking down the

209

idiot who thought he could make me disappear so easily that I hadn't even texted her.

She hadn't texted me either, and I began to worry.

She'd already tried to leave me once because she wasn't ready for something serious, because she didn't want to be involved with a man who always had a target on his back. We'd moved past it, but I wasn't sure if we would move past this. I'd never expected her to witness a showdown, and I was mad as hell that some asshole had made his move in front of my woman.

If she left me, that would be it. I wouldn't chase her, and if she tried to come back to me, I would tell her we were done. Regardless of how I felt about her, I needed her to be like one of my boys, someone who would be there through thick and thin, who had the spine to endure the pressure and a stomach to tolerate the acid.

It took her a while to text me back, even though I knew she was off work. ***I miss you too.***

Did she really? If I showed up at her apartment, would she dump me again? I shouldn't make assumptions when we hadn't discussed what had happened, but based on the way she'd taken off last time, it was fair for me to assume the worst. She'd already let me down once. ***I'll be there in ten minutes***. My driver was already around the corner from her apartment, but I wanted to give her notice.

Okay.

I stepped out of the vehicle and smoked a cigar on the sidewalk. People walked past, getting off work and in desperate need of a drink and a cigarette. I stared at the green door that led to her lobby as I finished my cigar, giving her time to prepare for my arrival. "Don't let me down, sweetheart." I stomped the cigar beneath my boot then went inside, and I made it to her front door.

I let myself into her apartment and found her in the kitchen, wearing the same outfit she must have worn to work, a tight pencil skirt with tights and boots, a long-sleeved blouse snug on her slender body.

She looked like a hot piece of ass, as always.

My body moved into hers like a magnet, and I kissed her as I held her close, one hand in her hair and one hand squeezing her tight ass, falling right back into old habits, despite the dread in my heart.

She kissed me back like she really did miss me.

When I ended the kiss, I swiped my thumb over her soft cheek and settled it on the corner of her mouth, her lips painted the color of her Bordeaux, her makeup dark and smoky, sexy. I stared at her for a while and forgot all the bullshit that required my attention.

Her hand went to my wrist, and she turned into my palm to kiss it.

As innocent as the affection was, it set me on fire.

She kissed me again then kissed the pad of my thumb, leaving a tiny mark from her lipstick. She gripped my arm with her other hand, like she wanted my flesh, my protection, my heat. Then she stepped into me and rose on the tips of her toes in her boots to kiss my mouth, to kiss me as if I hadn't just kissed her when I'd walked in the door, as if the appetizer just made her hungrier. Her arms circled my neck, and she kissed me with tongue and breath, like she'd been aching for me every moment we'd been apart.

No other woman ever turned me on the way she did.

I squeezed her ass before I lifted her into me and carried her into the little bedroom down the hall, the one with the slanted walls because she rented the attic loft since it was cheaper. I laid her on the bed, slipped off her boots and yanked down the tights and the thong underneath.

Then I pushed up her skirt and kissed her pretty little pussy.

She sucked in a deep breath between her clenched teeth and then gave a pleasured sigh.

I hooked my arms under her ass, and I kissed her pussy as hard as she'd kissed my mouth, happy to be reunited with the one woman who had ever set me on fire, who had a pussy more addictive than the best heroin I'd ever injected into my veins, the best coke I'd ever snorted off a whore's ass.

She dug her fingers into my hair, and she enjoyed it, slowly grinding into my face, her beautiful sighs filling her small apartment on the top floor. When she was close to the edge, her hands went to my wrists, and she squeezed me hard, silently asking me to stop.

I could eat her pussy all day, but that was never how she wanted to come, and that was just fine by me. I yanked off my shirt, ditched the boots, jeans, and boxers, and then moved on top of her on the full-size bed. She opened herself to receive me, squeezing my torso with her knees and hooking her ankles together at the top of my ass. I sank inside her paradise and squeezed through her slick flesh, reunited with the tightness that rivaled the strength of a clenched fist.

Her arms circled my neck, and I pressed my chest into her firm tits. Her mouth was to my ear, moaning at my thick invasion into her little channel. It was like our first time all over again, when she'd taken me home from the bar and fucked my brains out like she'd never get another chance to have me, when she'd embraced her pleasure with passion because she didn't care if she looked eager or desperate.

I wanted to take her hard from the moment I saw her, but now that I felt her underneath me, felt her want me desperately, I slowed down to savor it. To make it last. To listen to her breaths and feel her nails claw at my skin until the sweat made the cuts burn.

I sat at her round table in just my boxers. When I'd come over here in the past, the temperature had been frigid because she hadn't wanted to use her heater, but now it was actually warm, which told me she was putting her new salary to good use.

She came out of the bathroom after she fixed her makeup, makeup I ruined by shoving her face into the sheets. She'd put on my shirt, and she took a seat at the table, her hair soft because she'd brushed out all the tangles from my knots. "Hungry?"

"Always."

"I don't have a butler to make us dinner, but I can order a pizza."

I smirked. "Pizza sounds great, sweetheart."

She grabbed her phone and made an order on a delivery app.

I wanted to take her to dinner, but when she put on my clothes and even my socks, I could tell she didn't want to go anywhere.

She went to her cabinets and pulled out a bottle of wine and a couple glasses. She set the table with plates, utensils, and water, the vase in the shape of a woman's ass full of flowers pushed to the side so we could see each other.

I wished she lived at my house, was always there when I got home, was always there whenever I left. But I didn't ask her because I already knew her answer would be no. It would cause unnecessary strife in a relationship that had only recently become easy.

Well, until the other night.

She drank her wine then looked at me across the table. "You can smoke if you want."

Her apartment was too small. It would become hazy like a London fog. I grabbed the wineglass and took a drink.

She continued to stare at me, her chin propped on her closed fist.

"I'm sorry I haven't texted. Just been busy."

"It's okay... I get it."

"It's not okay. I should have checked on you."

She sat back against the chair and shifted her gaze elsewhere.

"How've you been?"

All she gave was a shrug.

Perhaps it was worse than I realized. "Talk to me, sweetheart." She'd always been a confident woman who didn't shy away from eye contact, so I knew something was amiss when she didn't look at me.

She swallowed, her throat shifting. "I've—I've never seen anything like that before."

I assumed.

"I'm not gonna pretend I wasn't scared to death, because I was."

"That's okay."

She seemed to be more forthcoming when I welcomed her uneasiness. "I watched that guy bleed out right next to me...when you stabbed him. It all happened so fast, and then it was over just as fast." Her eyes continued to focus on the surface of the table. "Does that happen a lot?"

"No."

Her eyes finally found mine.

"It's been a while since someone took a shot at me, especially in a public setting."

Her eyes flicked away again.

"I'm going to be honest. Another reason I haven't called is because I thought you'd tell me it's over."

Her eyes stayed down for a while, like the fear wasn't ridiculous.

I studied her face, watched her cycle through all the emotions my statement caused.

After a long beat, she spoke. "I was scared. I still am scared...if I'm honest. But I'm not going anywhere." She finally found the confidence to look me in the eye, with a subtle hint of uncertainty. "A week without you was far more terrifying than what I saw."

My expression remained hard, but everything inside me went soft. I'd hoped she would stay, but I didn't expect her to say those beautiful fucking words. Didn't expect her to punch me in the chest with them. This woman had slipped through my grip countless times, but the chase had finally stopped. She was tethered to me now, the two of us connected by an unbreakable knot, a bond that I'd had with my boys, but never a woman. It meant the fucking world to me to hear that, so much that I almost told her how I felt, even though I knew she wasn't ready for it. So I said something else. "I can't promise that won't happen again, but I can promise that I will never let anything happen to you."

Her eyes were on mine, vulnerable and emotional, and they seemed to believe me. She was beautiful when she'd shown she wanted me when I entered the apartment, but she was more beautiful now when she was open with me, when she didn't pretend to want me less every time she wanted me more. "Am I a complete idiot for actually believing that?"

I felt the smile tug at my lips. "No, sweetheart."

I returned to Adrien's estate. It was just before midnight when I passed the gates and checked in with his butler. When I looked at the wall where the wedding picture had been, I noticed it was still missing.

Instead of Adrien meeting me in the entryway as with all our other conversations, the butler escorted me into the living room. The TV was on and showed the news. Adrien was in an armchair in his sweatpants and t-shirt, his beard dark from skipping the shave for at least a week.

When he looked at me, his eyes were empty and glazed like he was either drunk or depressed—or maybe both. "Want a drink?"

I sat in the other armchair with the coffee table between us.

He had an empty glass on the table, just water on the bottom because the ice cubes had melted.

"I'm good."

He grabbed the remote and turned off the TV before he ran his fingers through his unkempt hair. The wedding ring he usually wore was absent from his left hand. He wiped the corner of his eye before he regarded me, looking half dead. "You want a drink?"

Fuck, how drunk was he? "You alright, Adrien?"

He propped his chin on his closed fist and looked at me, suddenly having lines around his eyes and looking withered like a flower that had been chopped at the stem. "What do you want?"

"I came here to see if you've changed your mind about the business. I have to report to Oscar this week, and if I give him the answer he doesn't want to hear, he's coming for your head. Reconsider, Adrien."

"Tell him to come. Like I give a fuck."

"Adrien, your life is a lot more valuable than money—"

"Is it?" he asked incredulously. "I lost the one thing that mattered...so nothing matters. My own family hates me for what I did. My father doesn't look at me the same anymore. Now that I'm free to fuck around all I want, there's not a single woman I desire except for the one who doesn't want me anymore."

I almost pitied him. *Almost.* "Just because you and Fleur aren't together anymore doesn't mean she doesn't care about you, Adrien. She doesn't want you dead in an oil drum off the coast somewhere in the Atlantic."

His eyes glazed over like he didn't hear what I said. "Work is all I have, and I'm not giving it up."

"Adrien—"

"I have nothing to live for. I love her with all my heart, but that doesn't fucking matter because now she loves you." He looked like he was on the verge of tears, about to cry in front of another man. That was how drunk he was. "I pleaded with her to give me another chance. Was about to get on my knees and fucking beg. And then she kicked my chest and cracked it in half and said she's in love with you. So it's over...it's fucking over."

I watched him writhe in pain, watched him fight back tears of weakness, but it was an out-of-body experience, my head floating in the clouds, my heart skipping beats several times in a row. A smile emerged on my lips no matter how hard I tried to fight it, an unstoppable smirk that reached all the way down into my chest. "She said that?"

He sank into the chair like he wanted to disappear into the cushions like melted butter. He stared at the blank TV screen without blinking as if he was reliving the horror of the memory behind his eyes. He was so drunk, there was no way he would remember this in the morning. If he were in his right state of mind, he wouldn't have told me any of this, wouldn't let me see him at his worst like I was his friend rather than his enemy. "Yes."

I walked into the empty bar. It had closed an hour ago, so the counters had been wiped and the floor mopped.

Luca sat alone at a table, a drink in front of him that he'd made himself. He was texting when I walked in, and without pausing his message, he addressed me. "Bring me one while you're up there."

"You already have a drink."

"Just do it, asshole."

I smirked and made two drinks, a scotch on the rocks with a twist. I came back to the table and placed the glass next to his half-empty one.

Luca finished his message before he set the phone on the table. "Cameron doesn't know shit, and Jeremy is a snitch and he still doesn't know anything. I know they must run in circles with Godric and those fucking psychopaths."

"And you'd be right." I took a drink then licked my lips.

Luca stared at me for a hard second. "You talked to Godric?"

"He didn't give me a name but confirmed what I suspected."

"There's gotta be something we can do to get your brother to talk."

I took another drink.

"We hit him hard, torture him, and get that answer."

"Luca, you know I'm not going to do that."

"Why the fuck not?" he demanded. "Your nutsack is the one on the line."

I took another drink, the glass almost empty already.

"Bastien."

"I'm not gonna do that."

"He knows who wants your head, and he ain't saying shit," he snapped. "He doesn't give a damn about you."

"But he won't cross that line, and neither will I."

He released a frustrated sigh as he dragged his hands down his face. "Now isn't the time to be honorable."

Penelope Sky

"My father deserved what he got. Not Godric."

His fingers returned to the glass, and he looked out the window as he did his best to calm down. "What happened with your dad anyway?"

I ignored the question and let it die.

Luca didn't repeat it. "Then what's the plan?"

"I don't know."

"You don't know..."

"I'll get him, Luca."

"You should be a lot more worried about this, Bastien."

I sat back in the chair and finished off the drink. Now I wished I'd made another and planned ahead like Luca.

He seemed to understand I wasn't in the mood to talk shop, so he changed the subject. "What happened with Fleur? Did she run off again?"

"No." I felt the smile creep on to my face, like an old friend that walked back into your life.

His eyes shifted back and forth between mine. "Why are you smiling like that?"

"Because I'm happy, asshole." When times got tough, she'd stuck beside me. Any reasonable person would advise her to leave me, but she chose to be unreasonable and stay. Chose me the way I chose her from the moment I saw her. "I'm gonna marry her."

The shock was quickly replaced by a look of horror. "I'm sorry, what the fuck did you just say?"

"Luca, you know what I said."

"Bastien, you've known the girl for three months."

"I'm aware."

"You sound crazy right now. Crazier than usual."

The smirk remained. "I know."

"Look, I like Fleur and understand your fascination, but this is way too fast—"

"I didn't say now, Luca."

He didn't even bother to hide his relief at that statement. "Oh Jesus..."

"Not now, but someday, she'll be my wife. And when that day comes, I want you to tell her this story. How the two of us sat in this empty bar at three in the morning, and I told you she was the one."

Chapter 11

Fleur

The man in black put a gun to Bastien's head and pulled the trigger.

"Ahhh!" I ducked down behind the table and shook like an earthquake struck me.

He yanked the table off then grabbed me by the arm. "This bitch is mine now."

"No!" I jerked up in bed and saw my dark bedroom, the curtains over the windows to shut out the light from the city. I panted as I sat against the headboard, my heart about to burst out of my chest. "Just a dream...just a dream." I felt my own heartbeat to make sure this reality was the true one. Tears streaked from my eyes and down my cheeks. "Wasn't real..."

I reached for my phone on the nightstand, and without thinking any of it through, I called Bastien. My mind was still in a haze, still asleep in many ways even though I felt wide awake. I knew I shouldn't call him, but I did anyway.

It'd barely rung one time before he picked up. "Sweetheart?"

His voice was calm and strong like always, so he was alive and well.

When I didn't say anything, he spoke again. "Talk to me, sweetheart." There was more urgency to his voice now. "Are you okay?" Men's voices were audible in the background like he was working, but he picked up for me anyway.

It took me a second to talk, like I was still suffering from sleep paralysis. "I'm okay... I had this dream... I don't know why I called you."

"You called me because I'm your man and you're scared. I'll be there in ten minutes."

"It's okay. You don't need to do that—"

"I want to do that, sweetheart." He hung up without saying goodbye.

I put the phone aside and continued to sit against the headboard, too terrified to go back to sleep, the images of the assault fresh in my mind. I could still smell the restaurant, could feel the cool tile against my hands as I kneeled on the floor behind the table. It'd been days since it happened, but it still felt like only a few hours ago.

I looked at the time on my phone. It was two thirty in the morning.

It took less than ten minutes for him to get there. I heard the front door open and close and then his heavy footsteps as he let himself into my apartment.

I turned on the lamp on my nightstand and saw him step into the bedroom. He pulled his long-sleeved shirt over his head and undressed, stepping out of his boots before removing his bottoms and crawling into bed with me.

He leaned against the headboard then enveloped me in his arms, blanketing me with the heat of a roaring fireplace. He dipped his head and pressed a kiss to the back of my head, one arm over my chest with the other across my stomach. The sheets were to my waist, so I was sealed in his warmth.

I hugged his arm and rested against his chest, his familiar scent helping me feel calm. I could feel his heartbeat against the back of my neck. He had no control over my subconscious, but just having him there made me feel safe, made me feel untouchable.

"Want to talk about it?"

"I had a nightmare...about what happened. They shot you and then came for me next."

There was a pause. "I'm sorry."

"I've never had a dream like that."

"Nothing happened. Remember that."

"I know, but..." It was the most terrifying moment of my life. It had only lasted a minute or two, but the fear and violence had a profound effect. Bastien had been outnumbered and caught unaware, and he still handled it.

"You should stay with me until you feel better."

"It was just a dream." I didn't want to burden him with my presence in his home, having me around day and night for however long I needed to feel better.

"You're having these nightmares because you're scared. Stay with me until you don't feel scared anymore."

"It's okay—"

"I wouldn't ask if I didn't want you there, sweetheart." He squeezed me to him, giving me a burst of his warmth.

I never felt unsafe in this apartment. Didn't see anybody in the building who didn't belong there. But Bastien was the man who made me feel safe, who chased away all my cares and worries.

"Come on." My oversized shirt had dropped over my shoulder, and he pressed a kiss to the exposed skin. He moved to my neck then the back of my ear. With every kiss, the tension left my muscles, the grip on my heart loosened, and I breathed easier. "Pack your things."

It was almost four in the morning when we entered his bedroom.

He carried my bag and suitcase to the closet, a place I'd never seen before. It was a walk-in closet where his jeans and shirts were hung on hangers and his shoes were on the bottom rack. But most of the space was empty since he didn't need it all because his wardrobe was so simple. Like I was in a hotel, he placed my suitcase on the table in the center and unzipped it, making it easy for me to access it. He hung up the clothes that I'd brought on hangers.

I stilled when I noticed all the guns mounted to the back wall. Handguns, rifles, shotguns...

Bastien followed my gaze but didn't comment.

I set my makeup bag on the counter in his bathroom and then helped myself to his drawer to find a shirt for bed. I never asked his permission to do that, but he never objected to it. Didn't seem to care if I went through his drawers, that I had access to his closet. The man appeared to have nothing to hide. "It's okay if you need to get back to work." He seemed to be up all hours of the day, sometimes awake during the daytime and sometimes up all night. Someone else would be devastated by the irregular sleeping schedule, but it didn't seem to bother him at all.

"I'm all yours, sweetheart." He tugged down the sheets to the bed and got inside.

I set my phone on the nightstand then joined him. "Ugh, I have to get up in three hours."

He spooned me from behind and squeezed me to him, his large size making the mattress dip underneath his weight and tilting me toward him. His face was pressed into the back of my neck, his gentle breaths moving my hair slightly. "You don't have to do anything, sweetheart."

"I can't not go."

"It's called a sick day."

"But my boss knows I'm not sick."

"But you're fucking him, so you can do whatever the hell you please." He kissed my shoulder. "You aren't going. We'll sleep in and go out to breakfast."

"God, that sounds nice."

He kissed me again. "Then it's settled."

———

When I woke up, it was past eleven.

I'd slept so well, without any nightmares, and it seemed as if that horrible dream had never happened in the first place. When I stepped into the bathroom, Bastien was in the shower, like he'd just finished his morning workout.

It was the first time I'd had my things at his place, so after I used the toilet, I stood at the counter, brushed my teeth, and got ready for the day.

He stepped out of the shower and dried off with the towel before he walked to me, buck naked with plump muscles from his workout, and he grabbed my ass underneath my shirt and kissed me. "Morning."

"Morning."

He moved to the other sink and started to shave.

I watched him in the mirror, stared at the tight muscles of his body, the lines that segmented the different groups under his skin, the way he was so ripped he looked like a living sculpture.

He caught my stare and met my eyes.

I looked away.

He continued to shave.

When I looked at him again, he had a smirk on his face.

I was careful not to stare again as I put on my makeup and did my hair. I was blessed with dry hair, so I could go several days without washing it and it would look exactly the same. Another reason I didn't work out, because why take a shower when I didn't have to?

We left his place and went to Holybelly, his favorite breakfast spot.

Like last time, the waiter talked to him about the most recent football game, the two of them going back and forth about the specifics of the match and the players. We ordered coffees, and Bastien didn't touch the menu, like he already knew what he would get because he always got the same thing.

"I'm glad I'm not falling asleep at my desk right now."

He was in a dark-gray long-sleeved shirt, the sleeves squeezing his arms in the areas where he was the bulkiest. His chest was broad and thick like a brick wall, and his shoulders were wide enough to carry a car tire. He didn't seem to hear or care about what I said because he didn't say anything, but he stared at me hard like his entire focus was on me, nonetheless. Then he smiled—seemingly out of nowhere.

"What?"

He gave a slight shake of his head then took a drink of his coffee. "Nothing, sweetheart."

"Nobody smiles like that for no reason."

It was a big smile, the kind that reached his eyes, like I'd said something particularly funny, when I hadn't said anything at all. "How'd you sleep?"

I didn't want him to change the subject, but I let it go. "Hard."

"Yeah, you were snoring."

"What?"

He smirked. "It was cute."

"I do not snore."

"Well, you did."

"I've never snored in my life."

He shrugged. "You must have been really tired."

"God...was I loud?"

He considered the question, the smirk still there. "A little."

"Oh no." I cupped my face because I was mortified, mortified that I'd sounded like a pig in a sty while this hot piece of man had to listen to it.

"It was cute, really."

"You're so full of it."

He chuckled. "I'm not. It really didn't bother me."

"Well, I'm sorry."

"Don't be." He took another drink of his coffee, still looking at me with that playfulness in his eyes.

The waiter came over and took our orders before he walked off again.

"Do you have dinner plans tomorrow?"

"No." I didn't have any plans ever, not after my life fell apart.

"Good. We're having dinner with my mother."

My ears heard exactly what he said, but my mind didn't accept it. "I'm sorry, what?"

"Dinner—with my mom."

"Uh...why?"

Instead of being offended by my poor response, he retained his smile. "I told her about you."

"Oh..."

He took another drink from his coffee, which he drank black.

"I—I'm not sure if I'm ready for that."

"Why?"

"What if she doesn't like me?"

"Why wouldn't she like you?"

"I—I don't know."

"If it makes you feel better, I don't care whether she likes you or not."

"Then why do you want me to meet her?"

His smile widened. "Because she's my mom—and you're my woman."

My heart continued to race in anticipation. I had been nervous when I'd met Adrien's mom, but that dread was unnecessary because we became close so easily. But Bastien's mother was different.

He smirked like my uneasiness was comical. "What are you afraid of, sweetheart?"

"Well, you said drugs were part of the family business…"

"And you think my mother is some kind of mob kingpin?" he asked with a laugh.

"No," I snapped. "But she might be really tough and rough around the edges."

He chuckled again like the suggestion was preposterous. "She's nothing like that. She's an elegant woman who wears pearls and scarves and plays bridge with her girl-friends. She's soft-spoken and wouldn't raise her voice unless absolutely necessary because it's impolite for a woman to yell. She's like a miniature poodle—harmless."

"Hard to believe a woman so meek raised a son like you."

"She wasn't the one who made me tough. My father deserves all the credit for that one." His smile disappeared at the mention of his father, his expression turning hard and cold once again.

It wasn't that I didn't want to meet his mother. I just hadn't expected him to ask. "What did you say about me?"

He paused before he answered, like he needed a second to move past the thought about his father. "She asked if I was seeing anyone, a question she'd asked me a million times, and for the first time, I gave the answer she wanted to hear. She's excited."

"That sounds like no pressure at all…"

The smile started to come back. "She could hate you and it wouldn't change anything, sweetheart. I'd prefer her to like you, but it's not a requirement. She just needs to accept that you're my woman."

He removed a lot of the stress of the situation, but it was still unnerving.

"Be yourself."

"Well, I can't be myself too much." I couldn't show her all the sass and attitude. I couldn't tell her that her son was the hottest piece of man meat I'd ever seen in my life.

His smile remained. "I think she can handle it."

We returned to his place after breakfast, and the second we were in his bedroom, he came up behind me and tugged my shirt over my head before he gave my shoulder a hard kiss. He squeezed me to him as he slid his hand into the front of my jeans and played with my nub in my panties, kissing my shoulder and my neck as he rubbed his fingers hard into my clit, suffocating me in passion and pleasure instantaneously.

He tugged off my bra and unbuttoned my jeans before he yanked everything down then lifted me out of them, my socks still on. He set me at the foot of the bed and stood between my knees before he pulled down his bottoms and thrust inside me.

I cried out because it was a lot of dick in a little amount of time. It hurt because he had so much of it, but once the pain faded, just the pleasure remained, and it was so damn good.

He grabbed on to the back of my hair and tugged as he thrust into me, fucking me hard from the start, smacking my ass until it turned red, making me his and making sure I didn't forget that.

———————

We had dinner at the dining table near the terrace, the view of the Eiffel Tower so special that someone would pay a lot of money to sit where we sat now. Gerard had the chef make us two different things, protein and vegetables for him and something full of carbs for me.

It was a quiet dinner, the two of us enjoying our food and wine in comfortable silence. I looked forward to this every weekend when I didn't have to worry about work, and it was nice to have it on a weekday. To see him for more than just a quick dinner or a hookup. I should stay far away from a magnet for violence and find a nice guy who wasn't a cheater or a criminal, but I was trapped in Bastien's force field.

There was no getting out now.

"Going to work tomorrow?" he asked.

"Unfortunately."

"You don't have to."

I wasn't a billionaire like him. Or even a millionaire. I had a couple thousand euros in my bank account at that very moment, and it was the most I'd had in a while. "I've got bills to pay."

"You still get paid whether you go or not."

I gave a quick roll of my eyes. "I'm not going to do that."

"I told you I'd pay you to be my woman. Best job you'll ever find."

"And I told you I want you for you—not your money."

That smirk came over his mouth. "But it would be fun to role-play, wouldn't it? You pretend to be my little whore, to do whatever I say when I say it."

"We're pretty much already doing that."

His smirk widened. "Touché, sweetheart."

"What about you?" I asked. "I hope I haven't kept you from your obligations."

"You're always my priority."

"But I'm okay."

"You're okay now. But you weren't okay yesterday."

"I just don't want to burden you—"

"My job is my problem, not yours. Don't worry your pretty little head about it."

I spun my fork in my pasta, getting a big helping before I placed it in my mouth. I normally ate very little, but all this good food that Bastien was giving me was making me eat nonstop and making my jeans a little tight. That first month I lived on my own, I hardly ate anything and lost at least ten pounds. Now, I was gaining it back far quicker than I'd lost it.

"So...did you get the guy?"

He was quiet for a while, just staring at me across the table. "I told you not to worry your pretty head about it."

"I know. But it would make me feel better to know he was dead." That he wouldn't come back for Bastien.

He didn't say anything. Didn't say what I wanted to hear to make me feel better. Let the silence speak for itself.

I was disappointed I didn't get the answer I wanted, but I appreciated his honesty. "Do you ever get scared?"

"No." He didn't have to consider the question for more than a second to know how he felt about it. "Death is just another part of life. It comes for us all in the end."

"But most people aren't shot dead in a restaurant...or stuffed in an oil drum."

"Whether you're stuffed in an oil drum or buried in the cemetery, it doesn't change the fact that you're dead. And the manner in which you died doesn't make a difference either. At least not to me."

I was shocked he could feel so indifferent to his own death, but I shouldn't be surprised by it. To live in his world, he had to be made of something different from the rest of us. He must not feel anxiety or fear...or anything.

"Or perhaps I'm not afraid of death because I know it's not coming for me—because I won't let it." His stare burned hard into my face, locked on me like I was the target of his aim. "Not when I have something to live for."

My instinct was to break the contact, to sever the intensity with which he gripped me, but I held on tightly. My heart beat a little faster. A little harder. My fingertips felt numb, my knees suddenly weak. "Promise me you'll find him."

"I will, sweetheart."

"And when you said this doesn't happen a lot...you meant that?"

"Yes. The Fifth Republic has rules that must be followed. But of course, there are always those who believe those rules shouldn't apply to them. These assholes emerge every few years, and after I stomp them to dust, it's quiet again... until someone else pops up. It's a never-ending cycle because these idiots never learn."

I nodded like I understood, even though I didn't understand a thing.

He looked out the window for a while, his beautiful eyes reflecting the lights of the Eiffel Tower on the Seine. He stayed that way, utterly still. "All my father ever cared about was the family business. It was the only reason he had sons, because blood was all he trusted. He took girls off the streets, from their homes, everywhere. He put them to work in our facilities, turning them into prisoners whose sentences would only end upon death. When I was fifteen, he said I was a man and ready to fulfill my role in the family business. He took me to the warehouse outside Paris. One of my classmates had gone missing months prior to that—and I saw her there."

I realized he was answering the question I'd asked a few weeks ago—why he cared so much about the rules. Why he protected women he didn't even know. Why it mattered to him when he had no daughters or sisters—that I knew of.

"When I tried to free her...my father made me shoot her."

My hand instinctively slid over my mouth to hide the quiet gasp that wanted to break free.

His eyes were still on the Eiffel Tower.

"He said he would shoot me if I didn't do it—so my brother did it instead." He spoke with melancholy, his eyes glazed over in old memories. "Shot her right in the fucking head... and we never spoke about it."

My hand finally left my mouth when the shock had passed. It was hard to picture Bastien as a boy when he was a six-foot-three man who could pick up a truck. Hard to picture a time when he was innocent and scared. But when I did, it hurt me. It hurt me so much. "I'm sorry, Bastien."

The sound of his name brought him back to me, his eyes connecting with mine again, still dead.

"Thank you for telling me that... I know that was hard."

He stared at me for a while. "It wasn't hard to tell you, not when I can tell you anything."

I didn't expect him to say that, and I didn't expect it to hit me so hard. His words slipped under my skin and hit all my buttons. He controlled my heart like a puppeteer and made me dance and sing.

He looked at the Eiffel Tower again. "I'm not a saint. I know how much money these guys are pulling in, and there's no reason they can't pay for the labor they need. It's a reasonable compromise, but assholes always get greedy."

"Did her family ever know?" Did they hope she was still alive?

"I told them she was gone and gave them some money."

"That was nice of you."

"Nice?" he asked quietly. "Shooting my father instead would have been the nice thing to do...and getting her the fuck out of there."

"You tried, Bastien."

He gave a slight shake of his head but didn't argue.

"I didn't know you had a brother." His family life was

shrouded in secrecy. He was open with me about every other aspect of his life except this one.

"Because I don't. Not in the traditional sense anyway."

"What happened between you...if you don't mind me asking?"

He looked at the Eiffel Tower for a while before he answered. "We have different ideologies. He believes in everything my father stood for—and I believe in the opposite. There were a few years when we came to a compromise and found a way to be brothers, but that went to shit. Now we're enemies, for all intents and purposes."

"Is he still in the business?"

"Yes."

"And I'm guessing he's operating his business against your rules?"

"Yes."

I nodded in understanding. "That's complicated."

"It is complicated. I have to stop him—but I can't kill him— and he fucking knows it."

"Do you think he's the one who...who tried to kill you?"

"No." He didn't have to think twice about it. "But he knows who did."

"And he won't tell you?"

He shook his head.

I thought I knew Bastien before tonight, but now I saw him in a whole new light. "What's his name?"

He looked at me again. "Godric. And I've spoken of him enough for one evening."

I could tell how much the strained relationship bothered him. How much it got under his skin and bubbled to the surface like a painful welt. "Can I ask you something?"

"Anything." His beautiful eyes looked at me, open and vulnerable, completely transparent.

"How—how many people have you killed?"

He continued his stare.

"You don't have to answer that question if you don't want to."

He considered the question in heavy silence, the seconds ticking by. "I can't give you a hard number because if I kill someone, then they mean nothing to me, and I don't remember people I never cared for. But it must be close to a hundred if I had to guess."

I swallowed at his body count—his *actual* body count.

"They were all bad men, if that makes it better."

I'd seen the way he'd taken out those guys in the restaurant with ease, even though he was outnumbered. He didn't need a gun when he was a killing machine.

"Does my answer bother you?"

"No."

"It seems like it does."

"It doesn't," I said. "It's just a lot to take in."

"Thank you for not judging me."

He was a criminal warlord who had danger inked in every one of his tattoos, but I found him to be the kindest, most wonderful man I'd ever met. "I could never judge you."

Chapter 12

Fleur

My heart was in my throat, and I couldn't swallow it back. I was normally calm and collected, but I was in such an unstable period in my life that I wasn't ready to make a good impression on anyone.

Especially his mother.

He said his mother was a classy woman, so instead of wearing something casual, I wore a skirt, tights, and boots with a long-sleeved turtleneck. I wore my nicest jewelry, a collection of rings and a gold bracelet.

Bastien was in a long-sleeved shirt and jeans, looking the same as he always did. "Ready?"

I sat in the armchair in his living room, wishing we could stay home for the evening and have a quiet dinner. My confidence had been shot ever since I'd moved out of my house. Once upon a time, I didn't care what anyone thought of me, and now I didn't know who I was anymore.

He watched me for a second before he took a seat on the edge of the couch. He didn't give me a lecture, just let me sit there.

I twisted the diamond stud in my earlobe, spinning it in place. "You're lucky you don't have to meet my parents."

"I'd rather you have parents to meet than have no one."

My fingers stopped playing with the diamond when what he said hit me hard. For a man of few words, he always knew what to say.

"Would you care if your parents didn't like me?"

I stared at him.

"If they told you to find a nice guy who wears a suit to work and earns an honest living?"

Someone who hadn't killed a hundred people. Someone who didn't tattoo his arms to hide his track marks. Someone who wasn't out all hours of the night because that's when the criminals roamed. Someone who didn't have twenty guns on display in the back of his closet. Bastien was the textbook definition of a bad boy, the guy who would make any mother scream, but I was in this for the long haul. "No."

That handsome smile spread over his lips, making him so damn attractive. "Alright, then."

The SUV pulled behind the gate of her beautiful estate, and then Bastien hopped out and took my hand.

I didn't know a lot about real estate, but her property had to be at least a hundred million euros. She was obviously very wealthy from the empire her husband had run before he died. I wasn't intimidated by her wealth, not after I'd stepped into Bastien's world of aristocracy.

The butler greeted us at the door and ushered us into the drawing room, where appetizers were already set out on the coffee table. Music played from the sound system in the ceiling, light jazz that was on so low it was barely there, just in the background.

"Madame Dupont will be with you momentarily." The butler gave a bow then left the room.

Bastien gave me a glass of wine and poured one for himself.

I looked out the back window and saw the gardens she had in the rear, ivy growing up the walls, sculptures surrounded by carefully manicured flowers.

"Is this where you grew up?" I asked.

"No. My mother sold that place after my father died. Couldn't live with his ghost."

I nodded in understanding.

"I like this place better anyway. I bought it for her. It was renovated a few years before she moved in, so it's practically turnkey. And it's a quiet neighborhood. Most of the neighbors aren't even in residence a majority of the time."

"So they just have these lavish properties because?"

"As an investment. Third or fourth home. A place to impress a mistress." He took a drink of his wine.

"Did your father have mistresses?"

He didn't acknowledge the question for a while, like he wanted to make sure his mother wasn't about to round the corner. "Unfortunately."

"Did that bother you?"

"If it did, he didn't seem to care." He took a couple of the appetizers in one hand and scarfed them down with his big mouth.

He always ate like a bear, and I found something about that so attractive. I guessed it was his manliness, how he needed to eat and eat because he was made of bricks and wrapped in human skin.

"Hello, dear."

I turned to see his mother enter the room, wearing a long-sleeved dress and heels, her blond hair done in soft curls, brilliant earrings in her lobes. For a woman who had to be in her sixties or seventies, she carried herself like a woman still in her youth, who could do yoga, go for a jog, who had a distinct vitality.

"Mom." Bastien quickly wiped the crumbs from his face before he greeted her, kissing her on each cheek. "Love the canapés."

She chuckled as she patted him on the arm. "You love food."

"You look nice, as always."

I watched his interaction with his mother, seeing how gentle, kind, and respectful he was toward her. The last thing I'd expected him to be was a momma's boy—and I loved it.

Bastien came to me, his arm moving around my waist as he showed me off with pride. Affection was in his eyes as he regarded me, like he wasn't the least bit nervous about the two of us meeting each other. "Mom, this is Fleur."

I extended my hand to shake hers. "Lovely to meet you."

She smiled, but it wasn't the same warmth she gave to her son. "Delphine. It's lovely to meet you as well." She pulled her hand away first and regarded me with a shrewd stare. "When Bastien told me about you, he said how beautiful you were—and he did not exaggerate."

Bastien smirked as his hand inched closer to my ass, his mother unable to see because she faced me head on. "I didn't need to."

"Are you two hungry? I haven't eaten all day."

249

We entered the dining room, a table big enough to host at least fifteen guests, and she took a seat at the head while Bastien sat across from me. The moment our asses touched the cushions, the staff emerged to pour our water and wine and provide our first course, a small salad with grapefruit, prawns, and tarragon sauce.

The initial meeting had passed so I wasn't as much of a mess, but my heart still palpitated with unease.

Bastien inhaled his salad then sat there and waited for the next course. "How are things, Mom?"

"Same."

"And Pierre?"

Pierre seemed to be a name of significance based on the way he said it.

"He's been well," she said.

Bastien looked at me and addressed the confusion he must have known I felt. "Pierre is her boyfriend."

"Not my boyfriend," his mother said quickly. "He's this gentleman that I've been seeing."

"Then he's your boyfriend," Bastien said.

"I'm too old to have a boyfriend, Bastien."

He rolled his eyes. "Not true, Mom. You're a very beautiful woman."

And just like that, Bastien made me fall for him even more.

His mother tried to hide the smile that wanted to creep into her features. She covered it up by taking a drink of her water.

"You should have invited him to join us," Bastien said.

"I didn't want to detract from the purpose of this dinner—meeting your girlfriend."

Bastien did not look like a man who had a girlfriend, but he didn't reject the label his mother gave. "Then next time."

"Perhaps," she said noncommittally.

I noticed she didn't eat much. She'd said she hadn't eaten anything today, but she still picked at her salad like she didn't have an appetite. The next course was a soup, and she only took a couple bites of that too, ignoring the bread in the center of the table. She was as thin as a rail and so petite, it was difficult to picture that she'd given birth to Bastian.

Instead of interrogating me, she talked about music and having tea with her friends and her favorite bakery. All the stress I'd had when I walked in here started to fade away when I realized she was a lovely person just like her son. Hard to believe she'd been married to a drug kingpin who exploited underage girls for free labor.

"I'm glad that my son's career choice hasn't deterred you." The tone of the dinner seemed to shift when the main course arrived, roast chicken with fingerling potatoes and sauteed kale.

I tried to gather my response, debating on telling her the truth or saying what she wanted to hear. "It's not ideal... but I know it's a package deal." Bastien told me he wouldn't give up his lifestyle for anyone, that if a woman didn't accept it, then she wasn't the right person for him. I wasn't sure what kind of future we had, but I didn't want it to end before it had to.

I kept my eyes on my chicken so I wouldn't have to see Bastien stare at me. I could certainly feel his look.

"Why does it bother you?" she asked.

Did she really just ask me that? "Well...wasn't your husband killed because of his work?" I looked up from my dinner to see her guarded stare.

Like she was surprised I'd asked that.

"I didn't mean to offend you," I said. "I just...that's something that scares me." I didn't tell her what had happened with Bastien in the restaurant a couple days ago. Didn't want to frighten her when she'd already been through enough. "Honestly, I'd rather be with someone with a more...traditional lifestyle, but..." I'd dug myself a hole, and I didn't know if I should try to go back or just keep digging deeper. "Bastien is the man I want." I kept my stare focused on her because I didn't want to see Bastien's face. I was dancing close to the sun, and I knew if I got any closer, I was about to get burned.

"You didn't offend me, dear." She released a sigh, as if letting old memories wash over her like a gentle breeze.

"Because you're right. It's something that troubles me every day. To lose a husband is terrible. But to lose a son... or more than one...is unspeakable. But this is the life the Duponts are destined for. We were always meant to live extraordinary lives. And with extraordinary lives come extraordinary risks."

"Was your husband already in the business when you met him?"

"This business goes back three generations," she said. "As the eldest son, he inherited this world. When we met, he hadn't stepped into the role yet, but my family was involved in the criminal underworld as well, so it was easier for me to swallow. Our marriage was supported by both families, a royal fairy tale in some ways."

"So this is the only life you know." I said it more to myself than I did to her.

"You could say that," she said. "It's given me a life I have no place to complain about."

I wasn't drawn to Bastien because of his wealth. We could live in my little-ass apartment, and I'd be just fine with that. With a man like Bastien to call mine, I already felt like a billionaire. "That's a good perspective."

"Bastien tells me you work at the investment company?"

"Yeah, I'm an executive assistant to one of his guys."

"He's gay," Bastien added like it was necessary to do so.

His mother tried to cover up the smirk that crept on to her lips. "Of course he is."

"He's nice," I said. "Easy to work for."

"Because he's afraid Bastien will kill him." Delphine said it with complete seriousness, no hint of a joke.

I sincerely hoped that was a joke.

Bastien didn't smile either.

"Bastien also tells me..." Her eyes drifted away as she tried to approach the subject delicately, like divorce was an ugly word. "That you and your husband are separated."

"Yes," I said. "We're getting divorced. He and I finally settled our differences, so it should be filed soon." I'd never told Bastien about my conversation with Adrien. I thought bringing it up now would make him ask for details, but he didn't question me, at least not in front of his mother.

"I'm sorry to hear that."

"I'm not," I blurted. "Honestly, I'm glad he cheated on me." Probably shouldn't have said any of that, but it just toppled out of my mouth.

Delphine watched me, clearly wanting to press for more but too polite to do so. "I have a number of girlfriends who are divorced. I've never heard a single one of them say something like that."

"*Mom.*" Bastien didn't raise his voice, but his tone was lethal.

"I just mean if he hadn't cheated, then I wouldn't have found Bastien," I said. "I've only known Bastien for a few months and it hasn't always been the smoothest, but I'm a lot happier with him than I ever was with whatever-the-fuck-his-name-is." After the last conversation I'd had with Adrien, I shouldn't harbor so much anger toward him, but even though I'd moved on with someone else, it didn't mean I wasn't still mad about what he did. He was my best friend, and he still betrayed me—and I'd never forgive him for that. For making me feel so worthless.

I felt Bastien's hot stare on my face, felt it pierce me with its intensity.

When I met his stare, he looked exactly as I expected. Staring at me so hard it was like the first time he saw me across the bar all over again. If his mother hadn't been there, he'd probably kiss me or bend me over the table.

I looked at his mother again.

"Then it sounds like you've found the right man."

Things had progressed far quicker than I'd wanted for a brand-new relationship, but we were too passionate and volatile to remain stagnant. We raced down the highway in a Maserati from the moment we met—and we still hadn't stopped for gas.

I didn't respond to that, too afraid to acknowledge what she said, especially in front of Bastien.

"Do you want children?"

"*Mom.*" Bastien intervened again. "Don't ask her that."

"Why?" she asked. "It's a harmless question."

"It's not harmless," he said. "It's packed with your agenda. You aren't as discreet or clever as you think you are."

Bastien and I hadn't talked about that. I wasn't sure what I wanted anymore. A couple months ago, I could have pictured myself with a brand-new baby in that big house, but now, kids were the last thing on my mind. We still had hundreds of miles of highway in front of us. I let her question die on the air between us because I really didn't know what I wanted.

Delphine returned to her food, sidestepping the tension that she'd caused.

I looked at my food, but I was aware of Bastien's stare. Felt the intensity of his look. Felt the way he reached across the table and grabbed me without touching me.

After dessert and coffee, we said our goodbyes in the entryway.

I thanked his mother for dinner even though she'd done nothing to prepare it—except pay for it.

"It was lovely to meet you, Fleur." The night started with a handshake, but this time, she gave me a hug and squeezed me tight.

I didn't expect her affection, not because she was a stiff woman, but because I didn't deserve it. I was practically a stranger to her, a woman who was still technically married to someone else while shacked up with her son. "You too, Mrs. Dupont."

"It's Delphine." She pulled away and gave me a smile. "I expect to see you again because my son wouldn't have brought you over if he didn't want you around for a long time." Her smile remained, enduring and kind. "And I'm sorry if I asked too many inappropriate questions. When you get old, your mouth has a mind of its own."

"It's okay," I said with a chuckle. "And you aren't old. When I first saw you, I couldn't believe you were Bastien's mother."

She lit up like a firework at those words, giving a laugh as she patted me on the shoulder. "That's sweet of you to say. But I can't take all the credit—not when my doctor and my aesthetician deserve it more."

"Bye, Mom." Bastien kissed her on the cheek before he grabbed my hand. "Thanks for dinner. Set up a meeting with Pierre so I can interrogate him the way you just interrogated my girl." He winked as he guided me to the car and opened the back door. He gave me his hand and helped me inside before he shut the door.

Delphine remained in the thirteen-foot-high entryway, watching her son walk around the vehicle with a slight smirk on her lips.

When Bastien got into the back seat beside me, the driver went through the gate and entered the quiet street that was devoid of traffic. The pavement shone from the rain that had fallen sporadically in the last few hours.

The stress was gone from my shoulders, and I suddenly felt light, like the worst had passed.

Bastien looked out the window, relaxed in the leather armchair, the ink from his tattoo visible past the end of his sleeve. "She likes you."

"She does?" I asked.

"You would know if she didn't."

"She seems too classy to be confrontational."

"She's the daughter of an arms dealer, the wife of a heroin distributor, the mother of two criminal sons. Trust me, she has no problem being confrontational when she needs to be." He turned away from the window and looked at me. "All you had to do was be yourself."

"I don't think she liked the fact that I was married...that I am married, technically."

"She doesn't," he said. "But that's not a reason to dislike you." He looked out the window again, and we spent the rest of the drive in comfortable silence. We passed the historic buildings with Napoleon's mark still present in the stone. Passed the cathedrals and the statues that made this city the most beautiful on earth.

We arrived at his home ten minutes later and took the elevator to the top floor so we wouldn't have to endure the insufferable walk up the three flights of stairs. The second he walked inside, he changed out of his street clothes, always wanting to be in his sweats or naked whenever he was home.

I was the same way, so we had that in common.

But the pajamas I used at his place were his t-shirts and sometimes his socks if I was really cold. I helped myself to his drawer like it was mine, pulled out a black t-shirt that smelled like it had just been laundered.

He was on the couch in his sweatpants and his ink was his t-shirt. He had the game on. It was the second half, and the score seemed to be tied. He'd already made himself a drink and lit up a cigar like he'd been itching to do that all night but would never do it in front of his mother.

He was too focused on the TV to notice me.

To notice the way I stared at the side of his face...and wanted to stare at it forever. The way my heart had slipped past my ribs and attached to my sleeve like a flag that blew in the wind. The way I missed him even when he was just feet away.

But he didn't notice any of that—and I was glad he didn't.

Chapter 13

Bastien

It was the shortest week of my life.

Fleur never felt like a visitor in my home. Habits and routines were formed almost immediately. She set an alarm every morning and let it snooze three times before she finally got out of bed. She never had breakfast, just had Gerard make her a coffee to go in one of the thermoses I'd never used in my life. He made her lunch too, and she told me she looked forward to lunch every day because she knew she had a gourmet meal waiting for her in the fridge.

When she came home and I wasn't there, she took a bath and soaked in the tub, enjoying chocolate-covered strawberries and a glass of champagne. As much as I wanted to stay home with her, I had too much to do, and I couldn't get distracted just because a fine piece of ass was now with me full-time.

I'd been living alone for fifteen years, didn't even have a roommate when I moved out, so I thought sharing my space with someone would irritate me at some point—but not with her.

I actually looked forward to seeing her every time I came home. Sometimes she was already asleep in bed, but I didn't hesitate to roll her over, fold her legs to her chest, and wake her up in the best and most savage way possible.

We had dinner together most nights. Watched TV on the couch together. Fucked in the shower, on the bathroom vanity, on the couch, and even once on the terrace in the fucking rain. If she just moved in and never said a word about it, I wouldn't say a word either. It would be an unspoken agreement between us.

But I knew she would leave—and I dreaded that.

The moment finally arrived when we were having dinner at Chez Georges. Sandwiched between two other tables and a room full of people talking about their day, we enjoyed our wine and bread as we waited for our entrees.

"I've been feeling a lot better," she said. "I think I'll go home tomorrow." She traced the edge of her wineglass with her finger, a mark from her lipstick visible along the glass. She followed the movement with her eyes just to avoid looking at me.

I didn't protest. Let her steer the ship—or, at least, think she was steering it. "There's no rush if you need more time."

"The nightmares have stopped. I don't really think about it anymore."

Would I be an asshole if I said I wished those nightmares haunted her every night? Just so I could be the one to chase them away. "Good. I'm glad you're feeling better. There's nothing to be scared of."

Her eyes lifted to look at mine, her dark hair tucked behind her ear, the low cut of her dress showing the cleavage line where my dick belonged. "Do you mean that?"

"Which part?"

"That there's nothing to be scared of."

"I'm the one they want, not you."

"And I'm not the best way to get to you...?"

"That's not how men like me do business. We leave wives and kids out of it. It's the code."

"Yes, that's *your* code. But that doesn't mean it's *their* code."

"Sweetheart, it's a universal understanding. No one is gonna do business with a wife-killer or a kid-killer. Because if you cross that line, then you aren't a respectable man. And regardless of the industry, you need to be respectable for anyone to work with you. Because everyone on this planet has someone they care about."

Her eyes stayed on me for a while, and then slowly, her shoulders dropped and she shifted her weight in the seat to get more comfortable, like she'd been on pins and needles just a second ago. "I really enjoyed staying with you. Thank you for letting me do that."

I wanted to ask her to stay, and if I knew she'd say yes, I would. "You're welcome anytime."

A little smile moved on to her lips. "It's a shame you have that big tub and never use it..."

"It's all yours whenever you want, sweetheart."

She chuckled. "So, I just come by every day after work and use it for an hour?"

"As long as you fuck me before you go, you know that's perfectly fine."

She chuckled again then took a drink of her wine, like she thought it was a joke.

I was dead serious.

"I'm excited to check my mail when I get home. The finalized documents for the divorce should be in there. Never thought I would be so happy to be divorced."

I wouldn't tell her I'd spoken to Adrien, not unless she directly asked me. I didn't want to involve her in our business affairs if I didn't have to. And I didn't want her to know what I'd learned either. That would probably just scare her off again. "What terms did you agree to?"

"I said I didn't want anything, and he let it happen."

If this were a couple weeks ago, I would have argued with her, but it didn't matter what she got in the divorce anymore. Not when she would be a billionaire somewhere in the near future, her only job to either ride my dick or suck it. "You can finally put this behind you."

"Yep." She took a drink from her glass. "It's been a crazy four months...really crazy." She stared at me across the table, looking at me exactly the way she had when she saw me walk into Silencio all those months ago, like she wanted to sink her teeth into me and carve her name into my flesh.

It was the craziest time of her life, but it was the calmest of mine. The first time I slowed down to listen to the raindrops pelt the windowpane in the middle of the night. The first time I drank wine to savor it. The first time I enjoyed being out of bed as much as I enjoyed being in it. My life suddenly had more depth to it, going from a shallow bank to a deep river. That kind of dedication should give my heart palpitations and tremors, but it gave me something else.

It gave me peace.

It was raining when I arrived at the house.

I had never made so many house calls for a single client.

The butler showed me into the drawing room, the same place where Adrien had slouched in the armchair, drunk out of his mind. The butler offered me a drink, which I took because I needed something strong to make this visit more bearable.

Adrien stepped into the room moments later, in a t-shirt and jeans, his wedding ring gone. He was subtly hostile but also indifferent to my presence. He took a seat in the other armchair, back perfectly straight, fully in control of his faculties.

I shook the ice in my glass before I took a drink. "You look better."

"Better than what?"

I sat back in the armchair and sized him up across the room, wondering if he really didn't remember our previous interaction.

"Adrien?" A woman's voice came from behind me.

I couldn't see her unless I turned in the chair, and I wasn't going to do that.

His eyes flicked to her behind me. "Wait for me in the car."

The sound of her heels came and went.

Adrien looked at me again.

Every other time I'd visited him, he appeared to be alone, his wedding ring his only company. But it seemed his attitude had changed. "You're moving on. Good for you."

He broke eye contact, like my words were sharp when they were meant to be soft. "Why are you here, Bastien?"

"Because this is the eleventh hour, Adrien. I'm meeting Oscar after this."

His expression remained rigid, like that information didn't matter.

"You weren't receptive to my last warning, so this is my final attempt to save your neck."

"Your last warning?"

He didn't remember anything, did he? I chose to disregard the question. "You don't know Oscar like I do. You don't know the Aristocracy like I do. They will not stop until each of your limbs is ripped from your body. They're proud of their history and their culture, and in their eyes, you're shitting all over it."

"I'm not breaking any rules—"

"*Adrien.* You've built a beautiful life for yourself. Retire or find something else. It's that simple."

He rubbed his palms together, his eyes on his hands.

"No amount of money is worth your neck." Did I really need to convince him of reason? Did I really need to father a grown-ass man?

"I've been in this business a long time, Bastien. People threaten me all the time."

"Oscar is different. He'll put a bounty on your head, and I promise you, everyone but me will roll on you. Take my advice and stop."

He lifted his chin and looked at me. "If you were me, what would you do?"

Probably jump off a bridge.

"You wouldn't back down."

"We're very different men, Adrien. You sell artwork on the black market, and I rule a fucking city. Don't compare yourself to me, not when I keep my word and you look your wife in the eye and lie."

He winced like my words were a spray of bullets.

"I don't give a shit whether you live or not, but my girl does. She's the only reason I'm sitting here."

"Does she know about this?"

"No," I said. "Just because you aren't married anymore doesn't mean she wants you to die a brutal death. If you don't have any other reason to step away, step away for her."

He looked at his hands again.

"Adrien." I felt my patience slip, like a teacher who couldn't get through to a student.

"If we were still together, I would give it all up to keep her safe. But I don't have her anymore." He looked at me again.

"I don't have anything except for this. And if Oscar is coming for me, that just means I need to come for him first."

I released an angry sigh. "Don't be stupid—"

"This is all I have."

I wanted to argue, but that was like trying to drive a Mini Cooper through the side of a concrete building. Fucking waste of time. I gave a slight shake of my head but said nothing more, knowing I'd done what I could. When Fleur realized that Adrien had been murdered, she would withdraw once again and halt the crawling pace of our relationship. My concern was entirely selfish, but I was a selfish man, and I wanted that woman so fucking bad. "Good luck, Adrien."

I met Oscar at the restaurant.

We were surrounded by regular people having dinner, unaware of the dangerous men sitting in the center of the room, having wine like civilized people when we were anything but civilized.

Oscar didn't say a word, staring me down like he wanted me to get straight to the point because that was all he cared about.

We hadn't even ordered yet.

"So?"

I gave a quiet sigh. "He wouldn't see reason."

His eyes narrowed, and he gave a slight nod in under-standing.

"Give me some time, and I'll try again—"

"No more time, Bastien. He's insulted the Republic of France long enough."

Chapter 14

Fleur

I hated my apartment.

Not because it wasn't a three-story villa with a staff of servants—but because Bastien didn't live there. He'd mentioned once that I could live with him, but I didn't think he was serious. It was way too soon for that anyway. I had to remind myself over and over that we'd only been together a few months, not a few years.

I threw together dinner in my tiny kitchen, watched some TV on the couch, and then went to bed in preparation to start the day over tomorrow. The curtains were drawn closed over the windows, but light from the nearby buildings crept in anyway.

In Bastien's bedroom, he had no neighbors because the Seine was directly in front of him, so only the light from the Eiffel Tower was visible—and I didn't mind that light one bit.

It was also colder in my apartment, and no matter how high I cranked the thermostat, it couldn't replace the warmth of Bastien's body beside mine. His big hands on my flesh. His hot chest against my back. The sheets were always cold because there was no heat to absorb.

I lay there on my side and tried to sleep, but then it started to rain. Having a loft apartment meant I could hear everything on the roof in detail, and the rainfall was like a thousand hooves from a stampede of wild horses. I loved the rain and didn't mind the sound, but it made me think of Bastien...and made me miss him like crazy. There were mornings we lay in bed together and watched the rain hit the window. Nights when he kissed me in it after dinner. Times when he would come over and his shirt would be slightly damp because he'd walked in the rain as if he didn't care if he got wet. There were times Adrien had come home and he'd smelled like a woman's perfume or cigarettes, but I'd just assumed it was a crowded room, that the guys had brought their girls. But Bastien only smelled like the rain...and nothing else.

My front door opened and closed down the hall.

I stilled in bed, at first feeling a jolt of fear at the thought of a burglar, but then I realized it wasn't a forced entry. Someone had let themselves into my apartment like they had every right to be there.

Heavy footsteps were audible on the hardwood floor as he moved down the hall and entered my bedroom. He was a shadow at first, but then he stepped into the strip of light that came through the slit in the curtains. Dressed in all black, his eyes brilliant even in the dark, he looked at me where I lay on the bed.

After a long stare, he undressed, pulling his long-sleeved shirt over his head and dropping his boots and bottoms. Then he crawled up the bed and moved over me.

My arms immediately encircled him and brought him close, my ankles hooking at the top of his ass.

He slid his hand into my hair, and he stared at me hard, his eyes absorbing my look with subtle desperation. He grazed his thumb over my cheek, tracing my bottom lip and the corner of my mouth.

I'd lain there missing him, and now that he was here, my heart ached in the most painful way. Like the emotion of having him there was somehow worse than the pain of missing him. "I missed you, babe."

His thumb halted mid-stroke, and his brilliant eyes locked on mine like his heart had skipped a beat. He possessed me with his stare before he cradled the back of my head and kissed me hard and slow, his lips moving with purpose, his fingers digging deep into my hair to get an iron grip. He made me feel like his without saying a word, just by gripping me and kissing me. The cold in the sheets was dispelled by his brilliant sun, and the longing in my heart was smothered by his masculine affection.

He reached for my panties and started to pull them off, letting me unhook my ankles from around his waist so he could remove them the rest of the way. He left my shirt on but shoved it up to expose my tits before he squeezed between my soft thighs again. He tilted my hips before he sank inside me, giving the sexiest moan when he felt me, like he wasn't skipping around town fucking all the women who made passes at him when I wasn't around. I was the only woman he bedded, and when he was in the mood, he came to my apartment in the middle of the night because I was the only one he wanted.

His mouth returned to mine, and he kissed me again, slowly rocking inside me, our bodies moving together with aching slowness, like we wanted to be together to feel each other, not get to the finish line.

I felt the hardness of his chest, felt the cords in his neck when my fingers grazed by, felt the hard bones in his jawline when I caressed him. With every breath, he breathed new life into me, made me feel secure in a relationship that was still in the early stages of blooming.

Before I'd discovered Adrien's infidelity, everything had felt right. But my relationship with Bastien made me realize it'd never been what it was supposed to be. We had so much depth, so much honesty, so much foundation. The passion and the desire and the chemistry were what brought us together, but everything else was what kept us together. Even if Bastien was a notorious criminal who was sometimes a drug dealer and sometimes a grim reaper, he was still the best man I'd ever known.

He lay beside me in the dark, the rain loud like falling stones on the roof. He had me pulled close, my leg hiked over his hip, his hand on my ass while his straight arm was my pillow. His eyes were bright even in the dark, his soul the source of their illumination. "Did I wake you?"

"No," I whispered. "I was just lying in the dark...thinking about you."

"Wish I could have seen that." A slight smirk tugged at his lips, like he wanted to walk in and see my fingers between my legs.

I felt a heat flush my cheeks. "Not like that. I was thinking about how much I missed you, even though I just saw you the other day." I lightly touched his chest with my fingertips, following the line down the center of his chest.

His smile slowly faded. "I always miss you—even when I'm with you."

My eyes flicked back up to his, fear and joy exploding inside my heart. Our car didn't have brakes, and it seemed to have unlimited acceleration. Every time we reached a new top speed, we were stuck there. I looked at his chest again and continued my scribbles on his skin. "Me too."

He didn't seem like the kind of man to say anything romantic, so when he did, it hit differently. It was authentic and real and straight from his heart. "Live with me." He hadn't blinked in nearly a minute, and the intensity of his eyes indicated he was too focused on my answer to do so. "I don't care if it's only been a few months. You have no attachment to this apartment. It's never been home to you, just a placeholder."

Months ago, he'd said I could move in with him for all he cared, but I'd never been sure if that was just a spur-of-the-moment reaction or an actual invitation. Now, my heart was in my throat, full of excitement and joy and also absolute terror. "Is it too soon—"

"For other people, but not us." His answer was so quick, it was like a bullet waiting in the chamber. "It's been fast because it's been right."

It had felt right with Adrien, and then he turned into someone I didn't know. I was an idiot to think it would be different with Bastien, but I believed it, nonetheless. Sometimes I told myself this was too good to be true, that this drop-dead sexy, committed man was playing a cruel trick—and I'd fallen for it. "You said you would take this slow—"

"I've been taking this slow." His eyes throbbed with desperate intensity, pulling me deep into his soul. "If it were up to me, you would have moved in with me months ago. If it were up to me, a lot of things would be different right now. But I've been patient like a goddamn saint—and I can't do it anymore. I want to come home to you every day. I want you in my bed every night. I want you soaking in the tub while I watch Manchester lose another fucking game on the couch. That's what I want—and you want it too. So, don't give me that shit that you aren't technically divorced yet and it's too soon and all that other nonsense, because what we have is fucking real."

We'd been lying together in the peaceful quiet while listening to the rain on the rooftop, and now it was contentious. When he'd come to me in the middle of the night, I was so happy at the sight of him, at the touch of his skin and the kiss of his lips. Sleeping alone wasn't hard after I left Adrien, but it was unbearable now that I was with Bastien.

His brilliant eyes continued to drill into my face. "It's a safe neighborhood and a nice building, but I don't want you here by yourself. I want to give you my palace and my security and everything you could possibly want—*so let me do that*."

"I don't want those things, Bastien. All I want is you—"

"Then move in with me."

He overpowered me in every conversation we had, the greatest salesman who ever lived. There was no pitch I could reject. I was scared to move in and get settled as his woman—and have him leave me for someone else...and then I would be back in an apartment just like this. Heart-broken and alone and broke. But I wouldn't bounce back, not like I had after Adrien.

He continued to silently demand an answer.

But I believed Bastien was different from Adrien. I believed in his honesty and integrity. And even though it was still hard to believe that a man so goddamn perfect could ever want me, I knew what I meant to him. "Okay."

The hardness in his stare immediately vanished, like he couldn't believe I actually agreed to it. "Is that a yes?" The confusion faded when he knew he didn't misunderstand my response, and then that handsome smile came through.

"Yes."

He smiled so bright, the smile was visible in his eyes. "Atta-girl." He squeezed me against him, and he gripped my ass as he rolled me over onto my back, his hand digging into my hair as his kisses smothered my neck. He pressed his mouth against mine, and he kissed me hard as he positioned himself between my thighs and sank deep inside me.

My gasp was muffled by his kiss. I gripped his back and felt the muscles harden underneath the skin. He rocked into me slowly, just the way he'd taken me earlier, the rain pounding the roof in the storm and streaking down the windows hidden behind the curtains. I used to hate the rain before Bastien.

But now, I loved it.

I came home from work and started to pack my things.

I didn't have a lot of stuff, but it seemed like I'd just unpacked everything and now I had to pack up again. My destination was a major upgrade and, if I was lucky, would be my forever home, but it was still hard to find the motivation to box everything up again.

I opened a bottle of wine, turned on some music, and got to work.

Bastien texted me. ***Are you done?***

The smile that moved over my face was instantaneous. ***It's gonna take me at least a couple days.***

Why?

Because I have a job.

Okay, then you're fired.

"This man..." ***Then it's going to take even longer because now I have to find another job.***

What do you need a job for?

Food, clothing, essentials...

That's what I'm for, sweetheart.

Thank you, but I can get my own stuff, babe.

There was a pause before his three dots appeared again. ***I love it when you call me that.***

The first time I said it the other night, it just flew out like the words had a pair of wings. I didn't know where it came from. I'd never called Adrien that, nor any other man in my life. I'd never used a nickname.

Just hurry the fuck up.

What's the rush?

Afraid you'll change your mind.

Guilt struck me like the blunt end of a hammer. It hurt because it was his truth. I kept him at arm's length because I was constantly afraid he would hurt me, but he was just as afraid of me hurting him. **I'm not gonna change my mind, babe.**

My apartment was full of boxes now. My clothes were packed away, which was the bulk of my possessions. I needed five boxes alone just for the shoes. Bastien said he would have his guys move everything for me, so it was nice I wouldn't have to do that part by myself. It was my last night in the apartment, the last night I would sleep alone and try to stay warm under the sheets.

Moving in with Bastien was a big decision, not just in our relationship, but in my life. I knew he was a dangerous man living a dangerous life. I'd seen men try to kill him with my own eyes. Even if he was the ruler of the city, the predator at the top of the food chain, I was still signing up for a life that was different from the one I'd always known. It was a risk, but Bastien was a risk worth taking. When he said he would keep me safe, I believed him.

For better or worse.

I was tired from working every day and then packing at night, so I went to sleep early. I normally went to bed at eleven and woke up at eight, but I was so tired I didn't eat much of my dinner and passed out shortly after nine.

I was dead asleep when I heard the sound of the front door.

I lay still for a moment, the sleep paralysis keeping me frozen in place. I fought against it, and then a smile spread across my face because I knew who it was. Tomorrow was when I was supposed to officially move in to his apartment —but he couldn't even wait a day.

The footsteps were audible in the hallway, coming closer to my bedroom.

I was so tired from working these last three days that I didn't even want to have sex, but snuggling with Bastien felt better than sex sometimes. The smell of his skin, the heat from his muscles, the way he could touch me so softly and then grip me a moment afterward.

When I heard his footsteps enter my bedroom, I felt my exhausted eyes open. "Couldn't wait another day?" My voice was quiet and cracked, my throat hardly able to work because I'd been asleep for so long. When I glanced at the clock on the nightstand, I saw that it was one in the morning.

He moved toward the bed, but he didn't undress.

That was when I realized there was another man in the room, moving to the other side of the bed.

The alarm defeated the haze of sleep as my fight-or-flight response kicked in. I pushed the sheets off me, screamed, and tried to crawl down the center of the bed to get away from them both.

I was grabbed by the arm and shoved down on the bed.

I screamed like my life depended on it. "Help! Help me!"

A gloved hand cupped my mouth and muffled my screams.

A needle poked me in the arm, and then the skin burned when something was injected into me. It took a second or two to kick in, but then I could barely stand, the world started to blur, and I found myself toppling face first into the sheets.

Then it was black.

I heard voices.

"Give me that list—or she dies." It was a voice I didn't recognize, but he was clearly the instigator because he spoke so calmly, like my life literally meant nothing to him. "I will bury her alive, and you can watch her suffocate."

I was aware of the cool tile against my cheek, of how hard the floor was. My eyes strained to open, strained to lift and fight the fog that was still potent in my blood.

"She's not my wife anymore."

I recognized that voice. Adrien.

"Let her go," Adrien said. "She has nothing to do with this, and you're violating the code."

"*I'm violating the code?*" the man asked incredulously. "You rob our museums and sell our artwork to foreign pricks, and I'm the one violating the code? Like the civilized man that I am, I offered you a pardon. All you had to do was bow out, but you're too much of a fucking prick."

Adrien's voice started to shake. "Then I quit. There you go."

The man laughed. "Doesn't work like that, Adrien. It's too late."

"I said she's not my wife anymore."

"But it's obvious that she still means a great deal to you. Don't play checkers with someone who's playing poker."

Adrien's voice was unsteady, like he could barely string a few words together. "I'll do whatever you want, Oscar. Make your demands."

My eyes finally cracked open. I could see the tile that I recognized, tile that I'd walked across barefoot for years. My eyes lifted to where Adrien stood, his eyes on the man who'd captured me from my apartment.

"You say she's not your wife, but you're awfully cooperative for her."

I couldn't see the man who spoke, but I wasn't sure I wanted to.

Adrien stood in jeans and a wrinkled shirt, like he'd been woken in the middle of the night to address this. That must mean only a few hours had passed, maybe even less than that. I kept my eyes cracked but was careful not to move so they wouldn't give me more of the drug. "What do you want?"

"I want a list of all your buyers. I want to know what they bought and how much they paid for it."

Adrien's tanned face suddenly looked pale, like that request wasn't easy to grant. "I don't have it—"

"Lie to me again, and I'll shoot her in the fucking head."

Oh Jesus.

Adrien lifted his hands as he spoke, a poor attempt to de-escalate the situation. "Why do you want the list?"

"That's my business, Adrien."

"If I give you that list, they'll come for me."

"Yes," he said. "But your wife—or ex-wife—will live."

This was the moment when Adrien was supposed to quickly agree to save my life, but he remained quiet, trying to find a solution that got him everything he wanted. He said he loved me, but when he had an opportunity to save me, he squandered it. "If I give you that list, they'll come for more than Fleur. They'll come for my entire family, my friends, everyone I've ever known."

"Yeah, you're probably right," the man said. "But that's a chance you'll have to take, because if you don't take it, she dies."

I was fucked.

Adrien started to pant, unable to keep his composure in the negotiation. "I'm the one you want. Let her go and kill me instead."

"No. I want the list."

"I said I would quit!" Adrien yelled. "I'll retire. I'll give you all the money I've earned—"

"That offer has expired, Adrien."

"Fuck you," he snapped.

"Fuck me?" the man asked. "Take her to the car, boys. And don't forget the shovels."

Oh shit. My body was still paralyzed. As hard as I tried to move my hands and legs, nothing happened. I could hardly blink. But I was able to move my lips, and I said the one thing that might save my life. "Bastien..."

Adrien heard me because he immediately looked at me.

The guys lifted me from the floor. I was scooped into someone's arms.

I couldn't fight the hold, even when my heart raced in fear. I was carried to the car that was on the property and laid across the back seat. One of the guys pulled out another needle to inject into my skin to keep me asleep.

With my last burst of energy, I said the only thing that might spare my life. "Bastien..."

Chapter 15

Bastien

I walked down the line and examined the containers of drugs, properly sealed so they could pass the border check inconspicuously. I picked one at random and set it on the scale to check the weight. It matched the amount on the sheet, so I knew no one was skimming anything. I returned it to the line and nodded to Horace. "Get it ready for shipment." I moved back to the table where the laptop was open. "Let's do the transfer." I logged in to the encrypted account and then turned the laptop toward Scott.

He entered the information and the total and then sent it before he slid the laptop back to me.

I checked that the cash was there and then turned it back to him so he could make his second payment. I didn't wait for the government to pay me out of their tariffs because I took my own. A lot of people didn't like it, but that was too fucking bad.

My phone rang in my pocket, and I checked it right away in case Fleur needed me.

It was Adrien.

I shoved my phone back into my pocket and ignored him.

Scott pushed the laptop back to me. "We're done here."

"Luca will meet you at the warehouse and take over the shipment." Luca got the international product to the docks so we could ship it to the Middle East and Asia. It was a whole enterprise, and it wouldn't be possible without the cooperation of our government.

My phone rang again, and I checked it.

It was Adrien—again.

"Asshole." I shoved it back into my pocket. Shit had probably gone down with Oscar, and now he wanted my help.

Nope. He was on his own.

I left the table and passed the line of workers who continued to process the batch of drugs that would go out in the next shipment in five days. When I'd arrived, it wasn't raining, but when I headed back to the vehicle, it was pouring. I walked through the rain and felt my shirt grow damp before I got into the back seat.

My phone vibrated with a message.

I pulled it out and looked at the screen, hoping it was Fleur even though it wouldn't be, not when she would be asleep at her apartment.

It was Adrien.

He has Fleur

He's gonna kill her

Fucking help me

Call me

These messages were popping up nonstop.

The alarm that shot through me was like an explosion inside my chest. My heart and lungs were ripped to pieces. I didn't understand the words, even though his message was clear. I didn't scream or shout, turned eerily calm like I always did when shit got serious. I called him and put the phone to my ear. "Head to Adrien's," I told the driver.

Adrien picked up right away. "Oscar said he's going to bury her alive. I don't know where he took her. He left a phone with a camera that shows her in a coffin."

"Where?"

"I—I don't know. He wouldn't tell me—"

"Where is he?"

"I don't know. He left."

I hung up and called Oscar.

It rang and rang and rang. "Pick up, asshole." It went to voice mail. I immediately called again, but all it did was ring.

It was intentional.

I called Luca.

He picked up right away. "I haven't received—"

"I need to find Oscar now. Call in all our favors. I want Oscar, and I'll pay ten million to the first person to tell me where the fuck he is."

Luca hesitated. "What happened—"

"He's gonna kill Fleur if I don't find her. Now do it."

I barged into the house and found Adrien sitting on the coffee table—sobbing like a little girl. "They took her. They fucking took her—"

I noticed the phone on the table next to him, the screen lit up with a video. I brought it to my face and saw Fleur lying in a coffin, her eyes closed like she was drugged. The camera had night vision, so I could see her in the pitch dark. There was no time to be emotional about what I saw, even though it fucking killed me. "She's alive." I'd seen enough dead people to know the difference. "And she's still under." She wouldn't have to know that she was buried six feet underground. "Come on, let's go."

"Where—where?"

"Shut up and get in the car." I headed back outside, and just before I got to the vehicle, Luca called. "Where is he?"

"I sent the information to everyone we know. Should have intel any second."

I slammed the door then looked at the roof. The rain started to come down harder, sounding like hail. "Fuck."

"What?"

"They buried Fleur in a coffin."

Luca didn't say anything, but that was because he understood that she had enough air to survive at least a day under normal conditions, but with rain like this, she would drown in a couple hours, maybe less, depending on the elevation and the soil composition.

"Get me Oscar, Luca."

"You know I will."

Chapter 16

Fleur

I woke up with a gasp.

Cold drops hit my face. I felt it around my feet, felt it underneath my back and neck.

I looked at the ceiling, which was just a few inches from my face—and saw the camera encased in a glass orb. It stared straight at me, the camera lens not moving from left to right, just still. "Holy shit." Then I looked at the wood that surrounded me...and realized I was in a fucking coffin.

Rainwater was dripping through the cracks.

And starting to pool underneath me, a couple inches deep already.

It would keep rising.

And then I would drown in mud.

I started to pant in terror, started to panic, started to slam my hands against the lid of the coffin, but it was solid like concrete because I was buried in the ground. I screamed and started to cry when I realized I'd just let more water into my grave.

"This can't be happening."

Adrien let them do this to me.

He fucking let this happen.

Did he hear what I said? Would he call Bastien?

"Bastien..."

I tried to steady my breathing, knowing I only had so much air trapped down here. The rain was slowly dripping into the coffin and filling it. I would either run out of air from breathing it all, or I would run out of air because it was replaced by water.

"Bastien..."

I didn't know if the camera could hear me, but I suspected it was video only.

He promised he would protect me.

He promised he would keep me safe.

"He's coming for me...I know he's coming for me." I closed my eyes and pushed the tears away. I forced myself to stay calm to conserve my air supply. "Bastien, I know you're coming for me."

I just hoped he came in time.

Chapter 17

Bastien

I called Oscar several times, but he ignored every one of my calls.

I sat in the back seat with Adrien, who continued to sniffle, and didn't say a fucking word. We didn't drive aimlessly through the streets, just sat in the driveway of Adrien's property. I waited for Luca's call like a fucking prayer.

Then he called—and I picked up before it finished the first ring.

He spat out the address, time of the essence. "Go to 3 Rue Quentin Bauchart."

I gave the address to the driver. "Do not stop."

The driver exploded out of the driveway and raced through the streets with the intention of running every fucking red light.

"I already dispatched a team."

"Good." I hung up.

Adrien gripped the handle attached to the ceiling so his head wouldn't slam into the window.

I reached under the seats and pulled out the guns and the ammunition. I handed him a loaded shotgun and shoved the magazine clip into my automatic rifle. I didn't check the video on the phone that Oscar had left for Adrien. There was nothing I could do for her right now, and watching her suffer would just make this harder. I didn't want to know if I was too late. I didn't want to know if I didn't have enough time to save her. I wanted to haul ass like I had the chance to get her back.

The driver slammed on the brakes when he reached the villa.

My guys were already there, armed and ready to blow the building.

I jumped out, and Adrien did too.

"Blow it."

The guys put the bombs on the gates and blew it the second I gave my command.

In a horizontal line, we marched onto Oscar's property and blew away all the security men who worked for him. We lined the doorway with more explosives and blew the doors right off the hinges, charring the walls with soot.

"Come on!" I ran in first without a vest, ready to kill every motherfucker in that house. There were men waiting for me, and I shot them dead without giving them a chance to say a fucking word. "*Oscar!*"

I moved through the house and made it to the main sitting room. I'd never been to his home before. We always met out in the open to protect our locations and privacy. There was smoke throughout the house from the gunfire. It continued behind me, my guys moving to other parts of the house.

Oscar stepped out, arms raised in the air. "You said you wouldn't interfere, Butcher."

"Where is she?" I walked up to him and shoved the barrel of the rifle against his chest.

"This is between Adrien and me—"

"She's my woman, not his." I struck him in the face with the gun and made blood splatter from his broken nose. "*Now tell me where the fuck she is.*"

He stumbled back from the force of the blow then wiped the blood from his face directly onto his arm. "I didn't know—"

I grabbed him by the front of the shirt and slammed him so hard into the wall he lost his breath. "*Tell me where the fuck she is.*"

He dropped to the floor, and he heaved with coughs. "I wouldn't have taken her if I'd known—"

I put the barrel of the gun right against the side of his head. *"Tell me!"*

He reached for his phone in his pocket, lying on the floor as he typed. He remained in that position, like he was too beaten to do anything else except just lie there. "I sent her location. East of Paris."

"Tell your men to dig her up."

"They've already returned to Paris."

"Fuck!" I left him there and ran out of the house, Adrien following me.

Chapter 18

Fleur

I was nearly submerged.

The water didn't fill the coffin as drops anymore. So much rainwater had penetrated the soil that it turned into mud, and it leaked into my watery grave. It came in from all sides, bringing the cold and the filth.

There was so much water, I was practically floating, my face touching the camera as I tried to keep my mouth and nose above the waterline. I tried to dig at the bottom of the coffin, to rip a crack in the wood so the water would soak into the earth underneath, but with the water level so high, I couldn't turn to do that and breathe at the same time.

"Fuck, I'm gonna die."

He's coming, he's coming.

Bastien is coming.

He's on his way. I know he is.

Or am I gonna die like this?

"Bastien...come on."

Chapter 19

Bastien

We drove down the country road at full speed, a hundred and twenty kilometers an hour in the pouring rain, the tires unsafe on the slick roads. If we died in a crash, I wouldn't be able to save her, but if I didn't haul ass like this, I wouldn't be able to save her either. "Turn right." I looked at the phone, seeing the dot on the map out in the middle of nowhere.

Even though there was no road and it was just a field of dirt, my driver turned and drove over the dirt and mud.

"Keep going."

It was a bumpy ride, over rocks and mounds of dirt, the SUV shifting and shaking from the uneven terrain.

The dot came closer. "Alright, stop."

He hit the brakes.

I got out of the SUV so fast I nearly tripped. I sprinted forward, spotting the fresh grave immediately, a pool of water sitting on top of it. "No." I grabbed one of the shovels Oscar's men had left behind and speared it into the mud. I worked fast, throwing mounds of dirt aside, moving quicker than I did with my sets with the bar and weights.

Adrien grabbed a shovel and joined me, and then the driver did the same.

"Fleur, I'm here!" I threw the dirt aside, coated in mud and sweat in the pouring rain, all of us working and panting to get the dirt off as quickly as possible. But the deeper we dug, the more the water pooled, and I realized her coffin was already fully submerged. "Fuck!" My fingers found the locked hinges, and I snapped them free with my bare hands before I pulled off the lid.

She was fully underwater, her body floating.

For the first time since I'd found out what happened, I let the fear hit me.

I was too late.

"No..." I scooped her from the water, her limp body ice-cold to the touch.

Adrien froze at the sight of her, in so much shock, he fell to his knees.

I laid her down on the earth and immediately started chest compressions, tears pooling in my eyes. "Sweetheart, come on." I pushed hard on her chest and didn't care if I broke her ribs. I pushed and pushed then sealed my mouth over hers to force the air into her lungs before I pushed on her chest again. "Fleur, come on. Please...fucking come on."

Adrien sobbed just like he had at the house. Fucking useless.

She suddenly jerked to life, gasping for breath as her eyes snapped open. Then she coughed, expelling water from her lungs.

I immediately rolled her over so she could get it out and not swallow it again. I held her there, her face away from mine, and that was when I felt the tears burn my eyes and break free. I listened to her cough and gasp, coming back from the dead because I'd fucking begged God to let her stay.

When her coughing subsided, she rolled onto her back and looked at the sky, feeling the rain pour down on her face. She turned her head to lock her eyes with mine, and she released a shaky breath, her eyes watering at the sight of me.

I scooped her into my arms and pulled her close, feeling the pulse in her neck against my thumb. I held her in the pouring rain, my chest aching from the way I breathed so hard, and I forced my tears to stop.

"I knew you would come for me."

We pulled up to my estate, Adrien still in the car with us.

Fleur said she didn't need to go to the hospital. She just wanted to go home, and by home, I assumed she meant mine.

Adrien stayed in the car, and I helped her to my bedroom. She was covered in mud, and so was I. Whatever clothing she wore before was impossible to decipher now because it was thoroughly destroyed.

She headed to the bathroom first and started to drop the muddy clothes on the floor.

I stayed by the door. "I'll be back."

She turned her head so fast. "You're—you're leaving?" Her tone was packed with ice-cold fear.

"I'll be back in an hour."

"But I want you to stay. I need you to stay..."

I couldn't stay even if I wanted to, not when I was so angry I could tear down his house with my bare hands. "I have to, sweetheart."

"I almost died—"

"And I'm going to kill the assholes who are responsible for that."

She finally understood and didn't ask again.

"Turn on the news when you're done in the shower."

"Why?"

"Because I want you to see what I did to them."

Adrien and I returned to Oscar's residence. My men still maintained control of the perimeter, and the police didn't interfere. Luca was there when I showed up, in his vest and with a shotgun. "You got her?"

I nodded. "If I'd gotten there a minute later..."

He gave a nod in understanding. "How do you want to play this?"

"Execute the men who buried her. Oscar is mine."

"Let's do it."

We strode into the house, the marks from the explosion still visible on the walls. His men were still dead on the floor, having bled out and marked the rugs and furniture.

Oscar hadn't tried to run and was where I'd left him, sitting in the armchair with dried blood on his face, like he hadn't even gotten up to clean it. He was holding his shoulder at a weird angle, like his collision with the wall had broken something. "Did you get her in time?"

"Yes."

He nodded. "I'm glad to hear it—"

"You violated the code, Oscar."

"I didn't know she was your girl, Bastien. I thought she was Adrien's."

"Whoever she is doesn't matter. Because the code pertains to all women, regardless of which man she's in a relationship with. You may not like how Adrien conducts his business, but that doesn't give you the right to abandon the code you vowed to honor."

Oscar got to his feet so he could meet my gaze. "Adrien had the chance to spare her, but he chose not to." His eyes flicked past me to where Adrien stood behind me.

I slowly turned to look at him, eyes narrowed. "Explain that."

Adrien shifted his gaze between us. "He said he would let her go if I gave him all of my clients."

I tilted my head, expecting a better explanation than that.

Adrien continued. "But if I did, my clients would come for me and my entire family, including Fleur. There was no way I could save Fleur, no matter what I did."

"You agree and then come to me. You don't let them bury the woman you love."

"It all happened so fast—"

"*I should fucking kill you too.*" Fleur had endured all of that because her piece-of-shit ex was too stupid to think on his feet. "She almost drowned in mud, and you're equally responsible for that."

"Bastien." Oscar addressed me gently. "I never would have come for Fleur if I'd known."

"What kind of fucking excuse is that?" I turned back to him.

"Yes, I violated the code, but I never would have touched someone who's important to you. You know I speak the truth. It was an honest mistake."

"No such thing as an honest mistake." I turned back to Adrien. "You cheated because you *wanted* to cheat." I looked at Oscar again. "And you almost subjected an innocent woman to a brutal death for your own agenda. Those are not mistakes." I stepped away and motioned to Luca. "Take him to the car. We're going to Notre-Dame."

Oscar didn't know my plan, but he knew that was where he would die. "Bastien, we've known each other for years—"

"Shut up, Oscar."

The guys grabbed his arms, and Luca zip-tied his wrists together.

"I'm sorry." He tried to come toward me, but the guys pulled him away. "I said I was sorry."

"*You're sorry?* My woman almost fucking drowned, and you're sorry?" I came at him and punched him so hard in the face I bent his nose in the other direction. More blood poured down his face and seeped into his mouth until he coughed it up. "I will burn you alive as you hang from Notre-Dame, and all of Paris will see you die the death of a traitor."

They started to drag him away.

"Bastien, please."

I ignored him and stared at Adrien, my next victim.

"The Aristocrats will have your head for this!"

"Then I'll burn them next." I continued to stare at Adrien and listened to them drag Oscar out of his own house and into the car.

I would thoroughly enjoy ending Oscar's life, but I hated Adrien far more. "If it weren't for Fleur, you'd be hanging right next to him, charred to a crisp and being pecked by the crows."

He held my gaze with a lack of confidence, and when the anger in my stare became too much, he looked away.

"You better get on your knees and thank her."

His ankles were secured to the rope that was tied to the gargoyle statue on the very top of Notre-Dame. We made the climb to the top, no one to stop us from doing whatever the fuck we pleased.

"Bastien, don't do this. How long have we done business together?"

I ignored him and grabbed him by the back of the shirt.

His hands were bound behind his back, so there was nothing he could do except twist and turn hopelessly.

"Bastien, please don't do this."

I threw him over the edge.

He screamed as he fell fifteen feet, face first toward the street.

It was five in the morning, so we only had an hour or two before sunrise. We had to do this now, to make sure the fire would burn bright like the anger in my heart.

"Bastien! My wife. My kids."

"You're lucky I won't do to them what you did to mine." Luca handed me the canister of gasoline. I twisted off the cap and poured the contents down the rope, watching it seep down until it splashed on his boots then doused the rest of him.

It got in his mouth and nostrils, and he did his best to spit it out, making his body sway slightly. "Bastien, come on. Don't do this. Don't fucking do this."

I pulled out the pack of matches from my pocket then lit one, a little flame at the tip.

Oscar had to crane his neck to look up at me. "No. Bastien, no. Come on, I'll do anything."

I dropped the match on the top of the rope, and instantly, the flames broke out and sped down the fibers toward Oscar. The blaze was ravenous for fuel, charring the rope. The second the fire hit his boots, he screamed, and then the fire engulfed the rest of him.

His earsplitting screams reached all of Paris, begging for it to end even though there was no going back now. He burned alive as he hung from Notre-Dame, a fire in the City of Light, a bonfire of treason and betrayal.

I stared down at him and watched him scream as he burned, felt the rage in my heart burn brighter as I watched him suffer, knowing my girl had suffered the same way when she'd run out of air and inhaled the water into her lungs. I felt nothing as I watched the flesh char over his bones, felt nothing as I started a war with the Aristocrats, my former allies.

I'd declare war on this entire fucking city for her.

He finally went quiet, his body still on fire and slightly swaying.

Luca came to my side and stared down at his body. "The rest of them will come for us."

"I don't care."

His hand moved to my shoulder, comforting me like I'd lost Fleur...because there was still a chance I might. I might have saved her, but I didn't save her soon enough, and whatever we had might not be enough reason for her to stay.

I wouldn't blame her if she wanted to leave.

I wouldn't stop her if she walked out the door.

I'd let her go.

The story of Bastien and Fleur continues in the next installment of the Fifth Republic Series: The Saint. ***Order now.***

Fifth Republic Special Editions

I'm so excited to announce the Fifth Republic Special Editions! These stunning hardcovers are designed for diehard fans like you. Preorder now at **this link**!

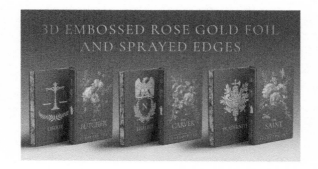

Follow Pene...

On the G: @penelopeskyauthor

And TikTok: @penelopeskyauthor

Made in United States
Orlando, FL
21 April 2025

60692342R00184